BUILDING STRENGTH

BOOK 9 OF THE SEAL TEAM HEARTBREAKERS

Teresa J. Reasor

BUILDING STRENGTH
A SEAL TEAM HEARTBREAKERS NOVEL

Contact Information: teresareasor@msn.com

Cover Art by Tracy Stewart
Edited by Faith Freewoman

Teresa J. Reasor
PO Box 124
Corbin, KY 40702

ISBN-13: 978-1-940047-33-1
ISBN-10: 1-940047-33-1
Print Edition

TABLE OF CONTENTS

PROLOGUE

THE DOOR TO the equipment room burst open. Lieutenant Sam Harding glanced up from sealing the bottom of each leg of his flight suit with duct tape. Seaman Elijah Nash, "Book" to the team, eased in, arms piled high with equipment, and with teammates Swan and Rosenburg hot on his heels.

"Think about it, Book. Two years is long enough, and you've already done that time. You don't want to hook yourself to someone for twenty, thirty, forty years when there are so many other…women out there just waiting to be fucked."

Swan had been trying for days to talk his twenty-two-year-old teammate into calling off his wedding.

Book dumped the equipment he carried at his feet and went to work on the cage combination lock, his straw-colored hair flopping over his forehead. "The whole point of finding the *one* is so you don't have to go out every night looking for a meaningless fuck, Swan. The gal at home is worth two on the barstool."

Book's Alabama accent was as thick as honey. He turned to face Swan. "Why are you so interested in my love life? You ought to be more worried about your own, because I don't know of you doing much fucking or anything else lately. A change of attitude might go a long way to remedy that."

The back of Swan's neck turned red.

Sam suppressed a grin. Book was like EF Hutton—whenever

he spoke, everyone listened, because he so rarely did so. He was everybody's little brother. He was amiable up to a certain point…until someone hit his stubborn streak. The kid's tone said Swan had finally hit it.

Sam hiked his pack over his shoulder and swung around the equipment cage. "Get that gear stowed, Book, and gather what you need. You know the drill. Swan that means you, too. And Squirrel—" His attention settled on Rosenburg. "Stow that bird-dog look and get your shit together. We're moving out in five, and I won't wait for you."

All three scattered to get their gear.

Sam had put off talking to Swan, thinking he'd lighten up, but it wasn't happening. The man had the bit between his teeth, and the closer it got to the wedding date, the more he rode Book's ass about it.

The SEAL had a real hard-on about marriage and commitment. He'd been burned, had a nasty divorce he hadn't put behind him, and now he lumped all women into the same category. As far as Swan was concerned, they were all untrustworthy bitches. But why the hell was he worked up about Book's wedding?

Unless he knew something about Book's fiancée.

He'd have to talk to Swan after the jump. And if he didn't know something important about her—and it would have to be something major—he'd tell him to lay off the kid or else.

Sam sauntered out of the equipment room, down the hall and out the side exit. Opening the back hatch of his Black RV, he shoved his pack inside and hiked a hip up on the ledge to wait for the rest of his team. Parachutes, masks, and oxygen tanks would be stowed on board the plane for them before takeoff.

Seaman Jeff Sizemore strolled across the parking lot, his flight suit already duct taped at wrists and ankles. "Hey, LT. Where is everybody?

Sam nodded. "Hey, Bullet. Stow your pack. I sent Denotti, Gilly, and Arrow on ahead to load the chutes and other equipment." He glanced at his watch. "And the others better jog out that door in about two seconds, otherwise we're leaving without them."

Bullet grinned, his dark skin looking coppery in the midday sun. He leaned back against the hatch frame. He was their FNG, Fucking New Guy, though he wasn't new to the teams. He'd transferred in after their last sniper cycled out and he'd slid in seamlessly.

"Good shooting yesterday," Sam said. The SEAL could shoot the eye out of a gnat at fifty yards.

"Thanks. It's my thing," he quipped.

"Seems to be." Sam shifted his attention from the exterior door to Bullet. The man grinned "Get in, we're going. They can thumb their way to the airstrip."

He was backing the car out when the exterior door swung open and Book shot through. Rosenburg and Swan caught the edge of the door, squeezed through together, and bounced off each other. Book slung his pack into the back, raced around, and got into the back seat on the right.

Rosenburg leaped in ahead of Swan. Swan shut the hatch and squeezed into the back seat. Sam purposely stomped on the gas, throwing the three back against their seats.

They were a good team. One of the best. But Swan was walking a thin line, and Rosenburg was encouraging him. That shit was going to stop.

THE C-130 HUMMED like a giant bee as it flew them toward the drop site. Swan and Rosenburg usually talked trash before a jump, but were silent behind him while they did their thirty on oxygen to leach the carbon dioxide out of their blood for the jump.

The pilot came over the bitch box. "Ten minutes out."

As he held the oxygen mask against his face, Sam scanned his team for any signs of anxiety. HALO—high altitude, low opening jumps—were always a little more hazardous than their regular practice jumps, which was why the guys were quiet and focused.

Orders for the exercise had come down from on high. What

did the captain have in mind? Were they practicing for an imminent deployment?

They'd just returned from deployment only two months before, but there was no guarantee there'd be four, five, or even six months between. If shit hit the fan, they could be called up any time.

"Five minutes out. We're at twenty-five thousand feet," the pilot announced.

Sam rose fitted his mask over his face and turned on his air. He wanted this shit behind him. "Fall in. COMs on, and check your oxygen." After everyone's thumbs-up, he said, "Sound off." Each man acknowledged him over his COMs. They'd have about a minute and forty-five seconds of freefall. Then they'd deploy their chutes.

The pilot warned, "Two minutes out." The cargo bay door lowered. The wind ripped at their clothes as it blasted through the fuselage.

Sam leapt as soon as the pilot announced they were over the drop site. There was a moment of weightlessness while the wind tore past him, and he took the knees and elbows bent position and turned to watch the rest of his men jumping. They'd fall in behind him as soon as he released his chute.

Like a topographical map, the land beneath him stretched sandy and hot, with sparse clumps of brown and green foliage. He lost the feeling of it hurtling up to meet him and relaxed into the jump.

Seconds flew by as fast as the wind. He checked his altitude and pulled his ripcord. The chute opened, filled with air then jerked him upward. Though he'd braced for it, he grunted at the sudden pressure around his groin, waist and shoulders, then worked the pull cords, directing the chute toward the drop site.

When his feet hit the ground, he ran forward with the momentum, the sand pulling at his feet, while he avoided the clumps of scrub and dried tumbleweeds. Where the air three thousand feet above had been cool, here the heat slammed into him like an open oven. Luckily he could see the transport truck fifty feet away.

He was already gathering his chute when Rosenburg's voice came over the COM, stress giving it a higher pitch. "Book's chute didn't deploy. He released his main chute and deployed his backup. Jesus! It released but... He's north of the drop site. He came in hard."

A rush of adrenaline hit Sam, and his heart leapt into a hard, furious beat. He dropped his pack and hustled to get out of his rig.

He clicked on his COM. "Book, come in." He paused to give the kid time to reply. "Report, Book."

Silence stretched. Thoughts about the wedding, scheduled for two weeks from today, crowded in, but Sam pushed them away.

Though he could see the men landing, he used his COM. "Team sound off as soon as you're down."

"Alpha two, boots on the ground," Swan reported.

"Alpha three, on the ground," Denotti replied.

Sizemore, Rosenburg, Aaron and Giles reported in.

Sam tried to push back against the compelling need to take action, forcing himself to wait for the team to converge on the transport. He gathered the parachute and other gear and slogged toward the transport vehicle to radio for both medical transport and search and rescue.

Already sweating in the neoprene suit he wore beneath the flight suit, he jerked at the duct tape sealing the sleeves and legs of his flight suit and tossed it inside his pack, then bailed out of his boots, gloves, and flight suit and peeled off the neoprene suit. Precious moments passed while he redressed.

Over the next twenty minutes the rest of his men showed up at the transport, stripped off their neoprene, and geared up for a ground search.

It would be like finding a needle in a haystack to locate Book. But at least Squirrel had seen him go down.

The crew of the transport passed out water while they waited for air rescue to show up.

But Sam wasn't about to wait any longer to search for his guy. "Pack water and fall in."

Each man grabbed two water bottles and clustered around

him. Sam accessed the Satellite Navigation GPS System. "Rosenburg saw Book's chute go down north of the landing site. I'm breaking the search area into a grid and we'll hoof it until search and rescue gets here."

He made the assignments using grid coordinates, pairing two men to a grid. "Anyone finds him, send up a flare and puff smoke. Our COMs won't work for long distances. You can fire your weapons to get someone's attention if the flare doesn't work."

"We can take you in closer, Lieutenant. Go slow in case we see your guy's chute," the driver of the truck volunteered.

"Thanks. Set your GPS to these coordinates, and we'll go from there."

They piled into the back of the truck. The men were silent, focused. Grim concern hardened their features. Swan's in particular. Was he feeling guilty for riding Book's ass about the wedding?

When the truck came to a stop, they bailed out.

The driver hung a hand out of the window. "No sign of the chute, Lieutenant. I'll stay here at the truck and coordinate with rescue."

Sam shot a thumb up. He'd purposely taken the farthest corner of the grid to search, and started the long trek at an easy jog, mindful of where he placed his feet, and keeping an eye out for snakes and hazards.

Sweat rolled down his face and soaked his hair and back. He stopped to drink a little water. After screwing the cap back on, he paused to search the area through the binoculars, and, like a stutter, heard the echoing beat of a chopper's approach.

A thin strip of white off to the west caught his attention. The sun and sand created illusions in the distance, making it hard to tell if what he was looking at was truly there. He stowed the binoculars and started the long hump in that direction. Watchful of snakes, he climbed the boulders piled one atop the other, blocking his way. The white parachute lay crumpled over the dry, sandy ground. It was Book's main chute.

"Alpha one to base." Static bounced back at him. He was out of range.

He swore in frustration and took a deep breath to shake off the looming anxiety. If Book had a chance, they had to find him fast, and it had already been almost an hour. He took out his binoculars again and looked north, spotting another small scrap of white. He stuffed the glasses back in his pack and leapt down off the boulder to circle around in that direction.

The heat was stifling, and more sweat rolled down his neck and into flight suit. He took another long drink of water from the bottle, stuffed it back in the pack, then picked up his pace.

The white object beckoned, offering a sliver of hope. Two helicopters wove back and forth in the distance, but weren't moving fast enough to suit him.

He recognized the billowing movement of parachute material and broke into a run. The chute was wrapped around a Joshua tree and partially covered Book's body. The urge to jerk the parachute away nearly overwhelmed him. He tried his COM system but all he got was silence. They were too far away from each other, and from the truck.

His breathing ragged, he approached Book, and with a sense of dread, gently teased the fabric away from the kid's body. Book lay on his side, the oxygen tank on his back holding him in place. Sam knelt in the sand and fed the strap through the tightening mechanism to pull it free without moving Book's head.

Where the mask fit tight against the kid's face red marks marred his skin. Sam pressed his fingers to the kid's throat and felt a weak pulse, then laid a hand on his chest and felt the faint rise and fall of his breathing. Book's skin looked pasty-white, and the leg of his flight suit was coated with blood, the sand beneath it rusty with it.

The kid was bleeding out. Sam needed to examine the injury and see if there was anything he could do. He took out his MK-3 Navy knife and slit the leg of Book's flight suit to find the neoprene dive suit had a hole in it, and through it protruded a bone.

Nausea ruptured his control, and Sam hunched over and looked away. God, if he breathed in the scent of blood he'd hurl.

He'd seen worse, but this was one of his guys.

After several deep breaths through his mouth, he fought back the reaction. He had no belt to rig a tourniquet. Using his knife, he cut a three-foot section of cord for the parachute. He wiggled the cord beneath Book's leg and through the sand so he wouldn't move it, and tied it around the kid's leg.

He jerked a limb off the Joshua tree, trying to break it off, but tore loose an eight-inch twig instead. It would have to do. He threaded the stick through the string and twisted it, cutting off the circulation to the limb until the bleeding eased.

Next he dug in his pack for his survival kit, flipped the hard, khaki-colored case open, ripped open a pack of sterile gauze, and covered Book's leg injury.

After making sure he'd done everything he could for Book, he extracted his flare launcher, loaded it, and shot one off, then pulled the pin on a smoke grenade and tossed it away.

Bright green smoke billowed up. Surely one of the choppers would see the flare or the smoke. Just as the thought came to him, one of the aircraft turned and streaked toward him.

The helicopter hovered, the downdraft kicking up sand. Sam covered Book's body with his own to protect him from the grit that whipped through the air and stung his skin. The chopper had barely come to rest when the door slid back and the crew leaped out.

Sam rushed to get up and out of the way of the medical crew.

"Is he alive?" one of them shouted as he rushed toward him.

"Yeah. But he has a compound fracture of the femur, and he's lost a lot of blood. I've made a makeshift tourniquet. He hasn't regained consciousness. He still had his oxygen mask in place when I found him. I removed it but didn't move him."

He watched while they assessed Book and alerted the hospital that they were bringing him in with possible spinal injury, possible internal injuries, and possible brain injury since the kid was showing no response to pain.

After immobilizing Book's head and neck, they cut the straps securing his pack, oxygen bottle and parachute, rolled him onto his side, and got him secured to a backboard. In just minutes they'd started an IV and readied him for transport.

Sam grabbed the back right handle of the stretcher and helped load Book into the chopper.

The crewman he'd talked to slapped his arm. "Coming with us?"

"No." He had to see the rest of the team transported back to base and write a report. But the rest of the team would go to the hospital as soon as they could change and head over there.

"You did good finding him. He may make it if we get him in fast." In seconds the medical technician climbed aboard and slammed the door shut.

Sam rushed to get away from the chopper, knelt in the sand and turned his face away as the rotor increased speed. The air tore at his clothes and created a stinging cloud of sand as it rose, and he only turned to watch as it shot forward toward San Diego.

It was while he was repacking his pack the adrenaline started leaching out of his system, leaving him shaky and nauseous.

He tried not to think about the list of possible injuries the medic had rattled off. Sure, he'd done all he could to keep Book alive until help came, but it didn't seem enough.

If someone had fucked up packing the chute, he'd find out. The seconds Book needed to ditch his main chute and pull the cord for his auxiliary would have been tight, and he could easily have run out of time. In fact, it was a freaking miracle he survived the landing. He'd need another miracle to survive those injuries.

Another helicopter rushed toward him and landed. The door slid open and Bullet leaped out and jogged to him. "This is our ride, LT."

"This is Book's gear. It all goes with us, and we have a parachute to recover a quarter of a mile back. I want a reason that main chute didn't open."

CHAPTER 1

O UT OF PLACE and underdressed, especially for a ritzy, high-society evening at the Hotel Del Coronado. Moira rolled her head on a neck stiff with tension and took a deep breath. Her off-the-rack evening gown, with its white lace bodice, three-quarter length sleeves, and pleated maroon floor-length skirt had seemed classic when she tried it on, but now seemed…plain.

She was a high school art teacher, not one of the businessmen and local politicians clustered in elegant, laughing groups around the room. And besides, she wasn't here to compete with San Diego's elite, but to accept an award for her school for raising twenty-five thousand dollars for the neonatal unit at South County General.

The soft roar of voices pulsed through the cavernous ball-room like a wave of static. The small string quartet onstage competed against it as Moira wove through the crowd and between the round tables, each with a beautiful centerpiece and set to seat ten.

Her attention was drawn to a man leaning against one of the pillars that separated the central part of the room from the bank of windows looking out over the bay.

If there was a reason for a man to wear a tux, he epitomized it. The dark jacket was tailored to his broad shoulders, the stiff collar of his shirt looked snow-white against his tanned skin, and his satin vest, embroidered with some kind of pattern, clung to a torso, lean but not skinny. And she'd bet there was muscle beneath that sexy, classy exterior.

His sharp, narrow-eyed gaze scanned the room as though he expected a fight to break out at any moment. His chiseled features were set in a frown that drew his dark brows together over a nose straight as a blade.

She itched for a drawing pad and pencil to capture that expression.

A woman approached him, brave soul. Though his features relaxed into polite lines, he didn't smile. They exchanged a few words.

Over top the woman's head, he looked up suddenly and pinned Moira like a butterfly to a board. Her heart leapt and her breath caught. Heat flared in her cheeks, and she pushed her glasses up the bridge of her nose before turning away to sit at the assigned table she'd finally located.

Elizabeth Travis, one of the hospital board members, and founder of Sarah's Dreams, took the stage and approached the microphone. "If everyone will please be seated, we'll get things underway."

Four couples found their places at her table. With her attention focused on the stage Moira sensed someone slipping into the seat to her right, but was distracted when the blonde woman beside her offered her hand. "Denise Clayborn, and this is my husband, Nelson."

As she leaned to shake the woman's hand, Moira's skirt brushed Denise's, and she noticed the colors were barely a half a shade different.

"It seems wine is the popular color this season," Denise commented.

"It would seem. I've seen several other dresses close to the same shade since I got here. It's very nice to meet you. I'm Moira McKee."

Denise had a friendly smile. "A strong, Scottish name, and you have the lovely red hair to go with it."

"Thank you." Moira touched the curling tendrils surrounding her face. She'd decided to not straighten her hair for this event, and was regretting it. No matter what she did to control the naturally curly mop, it willfully escaped every pin, barrette or ponytail holder, and fuzzed and curled at even a hint of rain. She'd managed to pin at least part of it atop her head and allowed the rest to curl down her back. "It's been the bane of my existence since I was born," Moira said with a grin.

The woman laughed. "And how long have you known Sam?"

Moira raised her brows. "Sam?"

Denise gestured toward the man sitting next to Moira, and she turned to acknowledge her tablemate.

Of course it would be him. Nerves jittered in the pit of her stomach. He wasn't so much handsome as he was compelling and very masculine. And he smelled delicious.

"Sam Harding," he introduced himself.

"Moira McKee," she said, offering her hand.

"Moira," he repeated her name, his tawny eyes fixed on her face. He had a tempered grip, neither crushing her hand to show dominance nor holding it like it was spun glass. Her breathing hitched at having all that intense masculinity directed at her.

"Are you still in the Navy, Sam?" Nelson asked, interrupting Sam's intent study of her features.

"Yeah." Sam released her hand.

"How many deployments?"

"I don't keep track."

The unexpected humility in the way he avoided answering caught her attention.

"How long do you intend to stay in?"

"As long as they'll have me."

"Well, your dad has two other Hardings to follow in his footsteps and pass the firm on to. And with your law degree, you can always transfer over to the Jag Corps when you decide you've had enough."

Sam raised a brow. "I like what I do just fine."

There was a bland note in his voice, but the heavy-lidded

glance he flashed in Nelson's direction had an edge.

"Moira, do you know Estelle and Joe Patterson?" Sam asked as he gestured to the couple directly across the table from them.

"No." She nodded to the couple.

"And Doris and Landon Thompson."

She leaned forward to nod at that couple as well. As she listened to him answer Landon Thompson's polite enquiry about his family, she wondered how a guy who hobnobbed with rich businessmen like they were neighbors had ended up a Navy SEAL. There had to be a story there.

Moira breathed a sigh when Elizabeth Travis called the crowd to order for the second time now that several guests had taken their places on the stage.

She recognized the mayor and the head of South County General Hospital from their pictures in the paper, and while she didn't know the other two, she was willing to bet they were going to pay for their meal before they got to eat it. Put four bureaucrats on a stage and every one of them had to make a speech. It was a given.

She reached for the glass of water at her place and took a sip.

"What do you do for a living, Moira?" Sam asked.

"I'm a high school art teacher."

"Tough duty?"

"Sometimes. And sometimes, when a gifted student lives up to his or her potential and gets a scholarship for college, it's all worth it."

"I can understand that. I'm in the business of pushing men to live up to their potential."

He had Navy SEAL written all over him. She'd have figured it out on her own even if Nelson Clayborn hadn't pretty much outed him. "Do you train them?"

"Sometimes."

She nodded. She'd read some articles about SEALs. If he wasn't involved in training, he'd be taking out threats in any number of places across the globe.

They fell silent as the first speaker, the mayor, rose and strode to the podium. He welcomed the attendees and gave a short intro about the history of Sarah's Dreams, Elizabeth Travis's nonprofit organization that raised money for programs to benefit hospitalized children. It was named for her daughter, who had died at eighteen months from complications during surgery to repair a congenital heart defect.

Moira had researched the woman and the organization before encouraging the student body to do the fundraiser. This year's project was raising money for the Neonatal Care Unit of one of the smaller hospitals in San Diego, the hospital where she volunteered.

The speeches went on, and she glanced over to find Sam watching her more than once. But he was way out of her league. His family must have money, plus he was an officer in the Navy. It didn't take a mental giant to see he was used to being in charge.

As soon as the last speech ended the crowd breathed a sigh of relief and a swarm of wait staff appeared with rolling carts and large racks and round trays to serve the meal.

"How did you get looped into coming to this thing?" Nelson asked from across the table, his attention focused on Sam.

There was a challenge in Nelson's voice that made Moira uncomfortable.

Sam shrugged one broad shoulder dismissively. "My father and brothers are out of town for a few days, and my mother asked me to come so I could deliver their donation and represent their law firm."

"I got looped into coming to represent my school as well," Moira said to the table at large, backing him up.

He leaned close and rested an arm along the back of her chair. She breathed in the clean, woodsy scent of his soap or cologne. "Maybe we can change a boring evening into something more interesting."

Was he really putting the move on her after only five minutes of conversation? The experience was surprising and new to her, and she stumbled around, searching for a reply. "I don't know you, Sam."

"You can get to know me when we dance later."

"I don't know how to dance, unless you count the jumping around like a maniac that everyone does in junior high."

His brows rose. "You're kidding, right?"

"No." She shook her head.

"No problem. I can teach you."

Her heart tap-danced against her ribcage in response to the velvety dark heat in his tone.

"I'm sure you're fast on your feet, but I like to move slowly."

He chuckled. That's all it took for her breathing to hitch, and she swallowed. His smile was as devastating as she expected it to be. Every inch of her skin seemed to have grown nerves she'd never been aware of, and every one of them quivered in anticipation of when he would touch her.

"I can do slow, Moira."

She squeezed her thighs together tight as sexual heat rushed to intimate areas of her body. Jesus! She bet he could do it all. And that was the problem. She'd feel safer cutting her teeth on someone who hadn't or couldn't. She was saved from replying when a waiter slid a plate in front of her.

Moira unfolded her napkin and spread it over her lap. The crab cakes looked delicious, but she was more than willing to eat now and pay for them tomorrow. She cut into the patty, and savored the bite, humming in appreciation while she caught Sam's quick glance.

She attempted to move the conversation into safer territory. "What do you do besides dance when you're not deployed?"

"If I'm not on duty at the base I run, fish, surf, and sail. I have a sailboat at one of the docks, and I take her out as often as I can. If you're interested, you could go out with me on Sunday."

"How do you know you like me well enough to be"—she almost said trapped—"on a boat with me for several hours?"

"The whole point of going sailing is to enjoy the wind, the surf, and the sun. It's peaceful out there. Though I bet with your beautiful pale skin..." He brushed his fingertips over her arm just above her wrist, igniting trickles of sensation along the path

"…you have to layer on sunscreen."

She swallowed. "Yes, I do. I wear my wet suit when I go to the beach for a swim so I don't have to apply sunscreen."

"Then you could wear your wet suit and a hat and not have to worry about the sun while I teach you a little about sailing."

To keep her mind from wandering to what else he could teach her while on his boat, she turned her attention to the last bite of crab cake on her plate, and just in time.

A moment later wait staff whisked away their empty plates and replaced them with their entrées. She'd gone with the chicken instead of the filet mignon because the crab cakes were the treat, but it didn't keep her from eyeing Sam's steak. She concentrated on the grilled asparagus to take her mind off the red meat. She'd come too far to backtrack now.

SAM STUDIED THE slope from Moira's shoulder to her breast. Shit, she was built—slender, compact, and all that glorious red hair… "What do you do in your spare time?"

"I'm an art teacher, but also an artist. I do work on commission. Plus, I swim every day at five before school, and I go up to the NICU unit at the hospital twice a week to cuddle the babies and feed them."

Alarm bells went off in his head. He wasn't ready for marriage or children. "How long have you been doing that?"

"Two years."

He paused in cutting his steak to lean forward and rest his forearm on the table. "Why do you do it?"

"Because cuddling benefits their development. Babies who are cuddled have better sleeping habits and are less fussy. And the parents who have to work, who can't be there all day to cuddle or hold them, need the extra support.

"When my youngest brother was born, I was twelve. He was premature, had lung issues and feeding issues. The doctors didn't expect him to make it, so they sent him home to die. But we held him constantly and fed him through a tube. He's fourteen now, strong, fit and plays baseball."

"So, you visit the unit and cuddle babies."

"It takes my thoughts away from school issues and focuses them on what's important, giving the babies the kind of human contact they need to survive."

"Plus, your school raised money for the NICU?"

"Yes. The kids really got on board and did several fundraisers. They've worked hard all year. I voted for a couple of students to come and accept the award on behalf of the school, but my principal wanted me to do it."

He turned toward her and his leg brushed hers. "I bet you had a lot to do with organizing the fundraisers."

"The students worked to make things happen."

Yeah, but he'd lay odds her organizational skills kept things running. "Moira, you inspired an entire school to get behind a project. That's no small feat."

She seemed uncomfortable with the praise and shrugged one shoulder while she chewed an asparagus tip, then took a drink. "The student body learned from the experience, and the school system got good press." And she'd also received several commissions because of the work. She turned toward him. "And what about you? Wouldn't it have been easier to be a lawyer than become a SEAL?"

He didn't really want to talk about himself, but there was something about her that elicited trust. "My father and I had a deal. If I finished college, I could do whatever I wanted afterward. So I went to college, finished in three years, enrolled in law school, and passed the bar. The next week I enlisted in the Navy."

"Was that the plan all along?"

"Yeah. I got the law degree in case I needed a backup plan some time down the road. I joined the Navy because it's what I always wanted." Had he ever told a woman all this?

"Did your father realize you were still going into the Navy?"

"He thought I'd change my mind once I finished school."

"When did you go into the SEALs?"

"Right after boot camp."

Her blue-green eyes rested on his face, her glasses magnifying their expression. "Would you say, then, that you're just a little bit of an overachiever?"

He laughed at her droll tone. "Maybe a little."

"And now you're a team leader."

"Yeah."

"A first lieutenant?"

"How do you know?"

"You have a law degree, so you came into the service as an officer. But you're not old enough to have been in long enough to have the rank of captain. What's your next goal?"

He captured one arrant red curl, finding its texture interestingly coarse, and guided it back into place down her back. Her dress had an intriguing V there that ended just between her shoulder blades, revealing velvety skin that was a temptation he couldn't resist. She froze as he brushed the back of one finger against the stretch of pale soft skin. "To get you out—" He paused and her heart leaped and hammered against her ribs until he finished the sentence—"on the dance floor right after they give out the awards."

She looked away afraid he might read her reaction and reached for her water glass again. "You may find you've bitten off more than you can chew. My size seven feet might feel like boat paddles when they step on your toes."

"I'm not worried. You're an overachiever, too."

She pushed her plate away, half the food still on it, and shook her head at the server when dessert was offered, then turned to Sam and raised one perfectly arched, red brow. Damn, but she was beautiful. "I'm not even in your league, Sam."

He studied her face. "I think it may be the other way around." Had he pushed too hard? And why the hell was he pushing like this?

Because she was the first woman he'd been interested in a long time. And all her soft, creamy skin was beckoning. Was she as soft all over as that strip down her back? Was the hair between her legs as red as all those curls topside? It took all his control to keep his gaze from wandering from her face to the generous breasts beneath the lace of her evening gown. "We can take a walk along the beach instead if you'd rather."

She bit her lip and her hand shook a little as she pushed the bridge of her glasses back up her nose. In that moment, she seemed…vulnerable and uncertain.

They both looked up as a tall, dark-haired young man paused next to Moira. "Mrs. Travis has asked that you join her for a few minutes before she gives out the awards, Ms. McKee."

Surprised, she hesitated. "All right." She rose and Sam rose with her. "Please excuse me."

CHAPTER 2

*G*OD, *I* AM *such a wuss.*

A handsome man was being attentive, and she was freaking out. Suspicious of his motives. Thrilled. Nervous because she'd never been good with social cues.

But she'd worked so hard to change her life, change her lifestyle. And now she was wary of anyone who flirted with her because she still couldn't believe they *wanted* to flirt with her. She'd had too many shatteringly painful moments in the past to completely believe in the good things when they came her direction.

Catching the young man's glance, she asked, "Do you know what Mrs. Travis wants to speak to me about?"

"Not a clue, but you don't need to be nervous. She's a nice lady."

She probably wanted Moira to convey her thanks to the student body for raising the money.

They came upon Elizabeth Travis chatting with three other people. "Here she is, Mom," the young man announced.

So, he was her son. How sweet that he described his mother as a nice lady.

"Moira, I'm so glad to finally meet you face-to-face," Elizabeth Travis said, then excused herself from the group. "Let's step out into the hall where it's quieter." She guided Moira out into the hall and paused there.

Elizabeth looked young for forty-five, but projected the poise and confidence of someone used to responsibility. Dressed in a pale peach gown with her hair up in an elaborate twist, she exuded grace as well. "I saw you're sitting with Denise and Nelson Clayborn and Sam Harding. I know Sam's mother quite well. He's a fine man."

"They've all been very friendly."

"I spoke to your principal, Mr. Jacobs, earlier in the day and he sang your praises. He said you were the driving force behind the students raising the funds for Sarah's Dreams."

"But the students did all the work."

"They certainly did an impressive job. The board at Sarah's Dreams was amazed they managed to raise so much money. And the donation was so unexpected."

"And the whole thing was a wonderful learning experience for them. Once we arranged for the journalism class to do a small documentary about everything the nurses and doctors do there to keep the babies alive and thriving until they go home, it just took off."

"A documentary?"

"Yes. I worked with their teacher, Mrs. Stein. As an assignment they created interview questions about the NICU unit. How it works, what the doctors and nurses do. They went into the hospital as part of the assignment and filmed the interviews. And they did a fantastic job.

"Also, every department and grade level in the school had a part to play in the project. The math departments helped keep the books for each grade and planned what the next project would be to raise funds. We had an open house and showed the video to parents, as well as the students' other planned projects. It became a year-long unit of study for the entire school. And the parents got behind it once they saw the interviews and some of the success stories that came out of the unit. They interviewed some of the babies' parents as well."

"That's...fantastic. I saw the news story the local station did on it, but I had no idea how wide-ranging the effort was."

"I hadn't intended for it to develop into so huge an undertaking, but once it snowballed, we didn't really have time to do anything but ride the tiger."

"All I can say is, you must be a really good salesperson to have gotten the whole thing off the ground with the school staff."

Moira initially proposed the idea during an in-service last summer, and by the time school started had done some research into what it would take to get it off the ground. "I had great people to work with. The teachers at my school want the best for their students, so they did the hard part and sold the idea to their kids."

"Would you be open to coming to my office one day next week so you could talk to me and a few members of my team about the project. I'd love for them to hear all about it. And could you bring your principal and the teachers with you as well? Say, Friday around six? I'll provide a meal for them all. Will a week give you time to pull them together?"

"Certainly."

"And as part of a thank-you to your school. We'd like to organize a small celebration for the students. I'll talk to your principal more about that after I've gotten together with my team on Monday."

Moira had worried about what they could do for the student body to reward them for their work. It would be such an anticlimax for it to just peter out, with no reward. "I'm sure he'd be thrilled. He's already mentioned doing something to celebrate their accomplishment. And we've already talked about doing a follow-up about how the hospital will spend the money. The journalism class wants to interview the hospital administrators about it."

Elizabeth laughed. "It sounds like you've created a monster. This is going to keep growing into other projects."

"I'm sure it will." The staff and kids were already talking about what project they were going to take on next year.

Elizabeth offered her hand. "I'm so glad we got to meet. I'll call the school first thing Monday morning and give you my contact information. You can call me on Thursday and let me know how many teachers to expect for the meeting and meal."

"Any time you say free food to teachers there's a stampede. There are fifty teachers, our principal and assistant principal."

"That will be fine. Bring the documentary. I want my team to see what teenagers are truly capable of."

"I will. Thanks so much for your interest. The teachers will be thrilled."

"What do you do during the summers, Moira?"

"I paint on commission. Mostly portraits."

"That's wonderful. Would you be open to doing something for Sarah's Dreams?"

"Certainly."

"We'll talk about that, too, when we meet."

"Sounds wonderful."

They walked back into the ballroom.

A tall man stood with Elizabeth's son near their table, the two males deep in discussion. The teenager broke away, his expression fixed and his jaw jutting with anger. He caught the hand of a slender young woman wearing a white lace top baring her shoulders and a wine-colored, floor-length skirt. He stalked across the ballroom, and whipped past them and out the door with the girl in tow.

The older man approached them at a more sedate pace. He appeared to be close to the same age as Elizabeth, but his hair already shone with silver threads at the temples, and his tux hugged his tall frame with the same immaculate style as Sam's. He slipped an arm around Elizabeth's waist. "Hey, Liz. Who's this?"

"This is Moira McKee, the art teacher I was telling you about. This is Mark, my husband."

"Nice to meet you," Moira extended her hand, and he shook it.

"It's time to make the award presentations, and then we'll open the dance floor. We'll talk next week," Elizabeth said.

"Thank you, Mrs. Travis."

"You must call me, Liz."

Moira's cheeks warmed. "Thank you." If Elizabeth Travis

could help them give the students some sort of celebration for all their hard work, it would be the icing on the cake for the school. And take some of the pressure off her and the principal.

Sam rose as she approached the table. He was taller than she expected, and it looked like his dark hair might have a touch of curl if it was longer. Walking back to him was a treat as well. He was handsome, driven, and sexy as hell, but she needed to be careful.

"Everything all right?" he asked.

"Yes. Everything's perfect," she said, giddy with relief and excitement.

His smile hit her down low. She needed to get herself under control. If she danced with him and he held her against that long, lean body, she might just experience her first orgasm. And that would be very embarrassing—and the perfect finale for the evening.

"YOU'RE A NATURAL," Sam said as he drew Moira in close and rested his cheek against hers, guiding her into a slow dance from the faster tempo of the previous song.

He'd been eager to get her out on the dance floor because it was the only civilized way of holding her close without propositioning her. There was something shy and self-contained about her, and those blue-green eyes seemed to delve beneath the surface of everything she looked at. She wasn't the type to jump into bed with a stranger after sharing a meal and a few minutes' conversation, and he'd outgrown that kind of behavior after his first semester of college.

"You're very patient and hardly flinch at all when I step on your toes," she commented.

He chuckled. He also enjoyed her droll sense of humor. "You've only clipped me once since we started dancing. You're doing fine." He eased her closer until her body brushed his. She fell silent, and he could feel her tension ease. He was hard throughout the song, and when it ended and they took a step back, her pale blue-green eyes rested on his face, all but inviting him to kiss her.

He was eager to do just that, but not in front of this crowd. "How about that walk on the beach?"

"I'd love it." She sounded a bit breathless. Good, because he was having a little trouble controlling his breathing, too.

They wove their way through the crowd back to their table. "I'll need to take the plaque upstairs to my room." She picked up the wooden trophy with its message of appreciation and her small evening bag, and they followed a group of people out of the ballroom to one of the main halls.

"You got a room for the night?"

"I've always wanted to stay at the Hotel Del, and I thought this function would give me a good excuse to splurge. It's steep for a teacher's salary, but…I couldn't resist. I plan to explore the hotel a little in the morning and take some pictures before I have to check out. And I hope you don't mind if I take the time to change. This dress and these shoes aren't really made for walking on the sand."

"Point taken." He'd go out to his car, get his go bag, and change too. "I'll meet you in the main lobby in twenty minutes. Is that time enough for you to change?"

"Yes, plenty."

They wandered through the hallways until they reached one of the elevators.

Just in case she changed her mind and left him stranded, he had to taste her. Despite the three people waiting for the elevator, he stepped closer, cupped her cheek, and took her mouth with a hunger that parted her lips as he drank down the hesitant response that built to something more.

She opened her eyes when he drew back. Her cheeks were flushed and her eyes dark as she searched his face. Her voice was husky when she said, "I'll only be a few minutes."

Would she rethink things and ditch him, or would she meet him in the lobby?

Five minutes later he'd collected his go bag and changed in one of the downstairs bathrooms, and had plenty of time to spare once he put his tux and bag in the car. So he found a seat in the lobby to wait.

He straightened a crease in the sleeve of his camo uniform shirt, a little wrinkled from being stowed in the bag. At least he was comfortable now, preferring his uniform to the tux.

He straddled two worlds. There was the rich, privileged world his father and brothers inhabited while running a multi-million-dollar law firm and entertaining themselves at the country club, yacht club, and social events like this one. And then he had his military world and the people in it, who had his back more than his family ever had.

And that brought him back to the reason he needed a distraction. Book was being kept in a medically-induced coma after breaking more bones than a veteran stunt man. And they still didn't know if he would ever walk again or be normal when he woke up.

The investigation into what had happened with his chute was ongoing. Par for the course when an accident occurred. In the meantime, jump schedules had been canceled, and every chute was being checked for problems. And his own team was going through the motions while they were a man down and their heads were fucked up over the loss of one of their teammates.

Didn't matter that the kid was everyone's little brother.

It was fucking with his head, too.

Moira appeared on the landing and crossed to the stairs. Surrounded by the rich wood of the stairs, the landing above, and the beamed ceiling, she looked too modern to be a part of her surroundings. She should have been wearing a Victorian gown instead of the white linen slacks, a flowing teal top and a windbreaker.

But she looked just as beautiful as she had in the evening gown, and he couldn't wait to touch the long tail she'd pulled her hair into and left curled over one shoulder.

The night was young. Maybe she'd invite him up to her

room…Mulling the idea, he went hard in a millisecond. He rocked to his feet.

She took in his military garb. "Something wrong?"

"No. I keep a go bag in the car. We sometimes get called up without warning. I didn't want to ruin the tux." He guided her down a hallway.

"How does your family react when you get called up out of the blue?"

His father rarely even remembered when he was out of the country. "My mother insists I stay in touch."

"And your father?"

He raised a shoulder. "Not so much. They're divorced, so he doesn't have her to remind him where I am."

"Yet you came to represent your father and brothers' business."

"My mother asked me to cover for my brothers."

She was silent a moment. "I'm sorry she put you on the spot. But if you hadn't come, I wouldn't have had a dancing lesson or a walk on the beach."

There was an unassuming innocence about her that made him feel protective. With her red hair shining like a beacon, some other guy would have found her and might not have behaved. The thought gave him a twinge he didn't want to analyze. "I'm glad I came to give you that dance lesson and walk with you on the beach."

He guided her out a side door to a concrete sidewalk leading to the beach. The exterior lights cast long shadows across the walkway edged with sod, and the hotel stretched down the beach in both directions. An area on the right, divided by trees, separated the Hotel Del's individual cabins, though the word "cabin" didn't exactly describe the well-built, white-sided structures that looked more like homes. On the left was one of the three pools.

Rounding the corner of the main structure, they stumbled upon a couple. His hands gripped her ass as though he were testing melons at the grocery store, while hers were fisted in his hair, and their mouths were locked together like they were superglued by the suction.

Sam looped an arm around Moira's waist and guided her off the sidewalk and across the grass toward the bungalows. The man raised his head, and the floodlight highlighted one side of his face and caught the gray in his hair, turning it to silver.

Sam recognized Mark Travis, but the woman he was with remained blocked by Mark's shoulder. Sam couldn't make out her features, though the dark red of her dress stood out like spilled red wine.

He and Moira remained silent until they reached the beach.

"That wasn't Elizabeth he was kissing," Moira said in a flat tone.

He'd seen that much. "No, it wasn't." Damn the man. He wasn't just fucking up his marriage, he was fucking up their evening, too.

"I wonder if Elizabeth knows."

Probably. "I don't know. I'm not up on the local gossip."

"I'm not interested in gossip," her tone sharpened. "I'm angry on her behalf. I've only met her once but... It's unfair to her. Disrespectful to her. Disrespectful to their family. I met their son tonight. If he knew what his father was doing... It would affect him."

Sam agreed with that. It had shaken him to the core when he discovered his father was having an affair. His contempt and anger had known no bounds, his outrage making him hungry for retribution.

He caught her hand and pulled her to a stop. "We can go back in and tell her what we saw, or we can let it go. Your choice." Telling her might be cathartic for them both, but people so often didn't want to hear the truth and sometimes ended up shooting the messenger.

After a brief pause, she shook her head. "We can't go in and tell her tonight. She's surrounded by too many people. I'll see her next Friday, and tell her then, after our meeting." They reached the end of the sidewalk, and the beach stretched before them. The sound of the water rushing ashore was like a whisper, and then a sigh as it went back out.

The soft sand dragged at their feet.

"You'll be seeing her?"

"She's arranging a dinner for the teachers and our principal next Friday." She stopped walking and turned to look up at him. "Damn him! He's a pig."

Pig was right. "She may already know, Moira. He's been at this a while."

"How do you know?" Her red hair was burnished by the distant lights, though her features were in shadow.

"They move in the same circles as my father and his wife. Mark has a reputation."

"If she knows, why would she stay with him?"

"There are probably numerous reasons. Her charity and her image might suffer because of a divorce. She's the CEO, but he accompanies her to present a united front to the donors. Or maybe she still loves him."

"Or it could all be about money," she said with a sigh.

Moira didn't seem to be the kind to be cynical about marriage or money.

On the other hand, he was cynical enough for both of them. He'd already witnessed the aftermath of breakups and divorces for all the reasons they both just listed. In the teams it seemed to be because of the long separations, injuries, money problems, unfaithfulness, and half a dozen other things.

Marriage was complicated by the people in it and too many external factors to think about.

Plenty of reason to avoid it.

She fell silent, and he let the subject drop, hoping she'd put it behind her so they could get back to each other. He was surprised by how much he wanted that.

"What were you thinking about while you sat in the lobby?"

Surprised, he glanced at her.

"You seemed angry about something."

"Not angry, just frustrated. One of my team was injured during a training exercise a few days ago. We're all waiting to see if he'll be okay."

"I'm sorry."

"So am I. Book was getting married in two weeks."

Her lips parted and her features stilled. "How horrible for him and his fiancée."

Book's fiancée, Alisha, was wrecked. And Swan was keeping his trap shut, but Sam had seen the guilt eating at him. He was going to have to have a sitrep with him soon.

"Book?"

"His name is Elijah, but he always has a book in his pocket to read during flights and downtime, so the guys call him Book."

"Do they all have nicknames?"

"Yeah."

She smiled. "What's yours?"

A smile threatened and he shook his head. "The guys don't call me by it. Not to my face. They address me as LT most of the time."

"What don't they call you?"

"Hard-ass."

She smiled. "I don't suppose it's because you have buns of steel."

He chuckled. "No."

"I suppose you have to be all business to make certain they do the job right. Their lives might depend on it."

"Pretty much." He didn't expect any more of them than he did himself. They had to be good enough for him to put his life in their hands. He had to be good enough to protect them. But he hadn't been able to protect Book.

"I wonder what my kids call me behind my back."

"I can guess what all the boys call you. Sexy Ms. McKee."

"I don't think so. I'm a bit of a hard-ass, too."

He laughed. "I don't believe it."

She brushed a strand of red hair off her cheek. "You've been warned."

She paused to look back at the cluster of cabins stretching out from the Del along the beach, their lights casting shadows over the sand. "Can you believe this place? It goes on forever." She got out her phone and took several photos.

After she finished, Sam rested a hand against the small of her back. "It's a throwback to another time. It was built in 1888, during the end of the Victorian Era."

"I've noticed some of the décor reflects that. How do you know so much about the Hotel Del?" She glanced up at him.

"I've lived here my entire life. And we do our surf passage training just up the coast. It's a navigational landmark we can see from out in the bay."

"I'm going to swim in the bay tomorrow, I'll keep that in mind."

"Do you swim every day?"

"Monday, Wednesday, and Friday. I go to the hospital on Tuesday and Thursday."

"And take the weekends off."

"Yes."

"Come sailing with me on Sunday."

She remained silent for a moment. "I've never been. What if I get seasick?"

"I'll bring some Dramamine."

She lapsed into silence again. "All right, I'll come. Where should I meet you?"

"I can pick you up."

She hesitated again, then offered her phone number and address. He grinned and keyed her information into his phone. Her phone dinged, announcing a text, and she got it out again. His number showed on the screen.

"In case you want to call me," he said.

They walked until the lights of the hotel were aglow in the distance, conversation easy and relaxed, then turned to retrace their steps. By then the surf had washed away their prints, and the wind picked up, making it hard to talk.

"It looks like a cruise ship all lit up, doesn't it?" she said as they approached the hotel, her hand gripping her out-of-control curls.

"Yeah, it does."

She took a few more photos, then secured her phone again. "Thank you for the walk."

"You sound so prim and proper, Ms. McKee." He could imagine that prim voice giving him instructions while they made love. He turned her toward him and kissed her, hunger running through him like an engine stuck in first gear. He wanted her to the point of pain. He gripped her ass and held her against him to show her how much while he nipped the sensitive area between her shoulder and neck. She shivered in response and she cupped the back of his head, urging him to continue.

When he drew back, her cheeks were flushed and her eyes looked dark and slumberous through her glasses.

"I have to go. I have to report for duty at zero-five-thirty in the morning." He waited to see if she'd invite him to stay.

"I'll look forward to the sailing lesson."

He couldn't decide if he was disappointed or pleased. It had been awhile since he had to work for what he wanted. But there was Sunday to look forward to.

CHAPTER 3

S AM ESCORTED HER back into the hotel.

She was such a fraud. She projected an image of confidence and control, but inside she was neither. She'd never in her life slept with a man the first time they met.

In fact she could count on one finger the number of times she'd made love. No, they hadn't made love. He'd fucked her and, being a virgin, she endured it. She'd been a pity fuck. The fat girl losing her cherry.

The humiliation of it had put her off of sex. Had put her off of all men for a long time. It was damn hard to open herself to that kind of pain again. Just the idea of being so agonizingly vulnerable again....

But she was different now. Inside and out. She was sixty pounds lighter. But she was still carrying the emotional weight of her experiences from before the weight loss.

Would being with a man help her shed some of the pain and self-doubt? And could she trust Sam?

He wasn't pushing. Wasn't handling her. But the way he left his arm around her waist, the way he tucked her hair behind her ear, the way he kissed her, jump-started something inside her no one else had even touched. Every nerve was poised for the feel of his hands on her skin, for the weight of his body atop her own.

She wanted him. Had felt that jolt of attraction the moment

she first saw him, but had dismissed it because before…he would never have looked at her.

He sure was looking at her now, though. And she wanted him to keep looking…and more.

But was she ready to be so reckless? Though her entire body was ready, her mind remained cautious. "I'll look forward to the sailing trip on Sunday."

"Wear something comfortable and bring sunblock, and maybe wear a baseball cap or sunglasses."

"Will do. Should I fix some lunch for us?"

He shook his head. "I'll take care of it. I know a place that does an excellent job. I have plenty of drinks on board, but I don't keep food because I don't know from week to week if I'll be there." He brushed her cheek with his lips, and when she looked up, planted a firmer kiss on her mouth.

He accompanied her to the foot of the stairs. "I'll call you tomorrow with an ETA."

She smiled at the acronym. "All right. Thanks for the dance lesson."

He grinned. "My pleasure." She watched his confident stride toward the entrance, and smiled as he turned and gave her one last wave.

She already regretted letting him go while she climbed the lobby steps to catch an elevator. But she'd done the right thing. She needed time to build her confidence before she took the plunge into a physical relationship with anyone.

She stepped onto the elevator with a couple, both blond, young, and unable to keep their hands off each other, though they were subtle about it. The woman clung to the man like a honeysuckle vine and ran her fingers up and down his shirt buttons.

The elevator door opened, and all three of them walked down the hallway in the same direction, and the two were already in a clinch before they got the door open. They stumbled inside and the door shut with a bang.

Was that how she and Sam would have been if she'd invited him upstairs?

To be with someone so strong and sure of himself, she'd have to project the same.

Even as she thought it, she reminded herself that she couldn't pretend to be something she wasn't. Otherwise the whole relationship would be based on a lie. She was just who she was. A slightly scarred woman trying to find her way to a new normal. If he couldn't like her for who she was… She'd regret it.

She let herself into the room, pulled out her keycard and phone, and placed them on the dresser. Shaking free of her windbreaker, she took in every detail of the room, from the pale gray hue on the walls to the darker gray curtains and comforter on the bed. Numerous pillows on the bed reflected both hues in their design.

She should have asked Sam to stay. She pulled off her ponytail holder and ran her fingers through the wind-tossed mop.

Her cell phone rang. She crossed to answer it.

Sam's deep voice came across the line. "Just wanted to be sure you made it to your room okay."

"Yes, I'm fine." She hesitated. "The room is nice. Secure. And I have a balcony. Have you ever stayed here?"

"No. I've only been there for hospital functions and a wedding or two."

She was trembling and her tongue suddenly felt clumsy as she said. "Would you like to?"

Silence stretched. "Someday or tonight?"

She'd just lost her mind. But their time together had been perfect. "Tonight." She was gripping the phone so hard her fingers ached.

"What's your room number?"

She could barely get it out.

"I'll be there in fifteen minutes."

She couldn't tell if she was going to die of embarrassment or anticipation. What would he think of her?

And she hadn't brought any sexy underwear or even a nice gown. He probably wouldn't even care about that. He wasn't coming back to sleep. The thought sent a rush of heat to her face that seemed to sweep over the rest of her. She was either making a horrible mistake or an impulsive, perfect decision. She'd find out which once he got here.

Her body was already warming, and the persistent, empty ache between her thighs was driving her crazy. Her breathing grew uneven and labored. She rubbed her hands over her arms and paced the floor.

At his soft knock her heart actually leapt, and she moved to open the door.

His eyes looked dark and his cheeks were flushed. Her own cheeks went hot.

She stepped back to allow him to enter the room, shut the door, and leaned back against it so her shaky legs wouldn't give out on her. Her throat went dry. She bit her lip. "I've never done anything like this before."

"I know. It's driving me crazy." He cradled her face in his hands and bent his head to kiss her with a care and gentleness that made the throb of need intensify.

When he raised his head, she was slow to open her eyes. "I don't have any condoms."

"I got it covered." He pulled his wallet out of his back pocket, opened it, and extracted two condoms. "Emergency stash. I've been carrying them around for over a year. Let's hope they're still good."

A laugh burst out, surprising her.

His grin pushed her need up a notch.

"Sam." Was that her voice with the plea in it?

He kissed her again, and the flick of his tongue against hers, the way his hands molded her against him, the way his body responded to hers, sent her own need higher.

Her hands trembled as she struggled to unbutton his shirt, and he rushed to help and shook free of it. She ran her palms over his T-shirt-covered pecs, and he stripped the T-shirt off too. She thought he might be the most perfectly formed man she'd ever seen. Muscles bulged in his shoulders, his upper arms, between his shoulders and neck. His abdomen was a thing of beauty, each muscle defined. She brushed her fingertips over each one, and they quivered and contracted beneath her touch.

He reached for the hem of her blouse and raised it, and she lifted her arms. Next he made quick work of the strapless bra she left on after changing out of her gown. Conscious of the white stretch marks on her breasts from before her weight loss, she fought the urge to hide against him.

The brush of her nipples made her shiver. He caressed one bare breast and kneaded it, and sweet pleasure pierced her. She put her arms around him and pressed her body against his.

Sam sucked in a breath and nibbled lightly on a sensitive spot between her neck and shoulder, then nipped the skin there.

She shivered again at the sensation, and her hands shook when she tried to unbutton his camo pants. "I'm a little nervous."

"It's okay, Moira. I won't do anything you don't want me to."

His deep voice caressed her with that promise, and her legs went weak.

Before she could get to his zipper, he bent, swept her up, and carried her to the bed. "I intend to do some undressing of my own."

He sat her in the center of the bed, then paused long enough to shed his boots and pants and placed the two condoms on the nightstand. His boxer briefs did nothing to hide his rampant arousal, and her body responded with an aching rush of need while her mind was thrust back to the pain and humiliation of her first experience.

But she was different now. And Sam wasn't anything like that asshole from college. This was going to be okay. When she reached for the button at the waist of her pants, he brushed her hands away and slid onto the bed with her.

"Let me do it." One-handed he unbuttoned her pants and slid down the zipper. "Your skin's so pale. Like warm cream." He laid his hand on the flat plane of her stomach. His skin looked dark against her own, his hand large enough to cover the space from pelvic bone to pelvic bone. The warmth seemed to build beneath the pressure of his palm just resting there. "At dinner I wondered if the hair down here would be as red as the rest."

That he'd been thinking that within the first few moments after they met sent a tide of heat to her face, but also fed the rising excitement that seemed to be wrapping her in a hormone-driven haze. The focal point of need between her legs ramped up to almost unbearable.

Her voice was swallowed to a whisper as she said, "You can look and see."

His toffee-tinted eyes looked almost black. "I want to touch first." He lowered his mouth to hers, his lips and tongue tempting her even as his fingers toyed with the elastic band at the top of her panties. Then his fingers worked beneath the fabric, gliding downward, cupping her so his fingertips grazed the most intimate heart of her.

Her hips rose instinctively, and her legs parted.

His lips left hers to nibble at her ear, his breath hot. "You're so wet for me."

She was going to die if he didn't touch her some more, and right now.

Using one finger, he tempted and teased, delved inside her. She gasped and couldn't keep still beneath the agonizing pleasure building until it tipped her over into a sweet, sweeping orgasm that rolled through her, leaving her fingers and toes tingling.

She was still trying to gather her wits when he withdrew his hand and peeled her slacks and panties away, shucked his briefs, and covered his erection with a condom.

For one brief moment she tensed as he rose above her. Her first experience hadn't been anything like pleasurable. But any lingering apprehension melted away as, with one smooth thrust, he slid into her. She caught her breath as the sensation of being filled overtook her and another, gentler orgasm rocked through her.

HE'D NEVER KNOWN a woman to be so sensitive to his touch.

She was shy and sensual. Plus, that thatch of red hair between her thighs *was* as fiery as the hair on her head, and he found it sexy as hell. And he'd seen few things as satisfying or arousing as Moira tipping over into orgasm.

As her body gripped him it took all his control not to tumble over into release. Her hands ran up his back, then down over the cheeks of his ass, and he nearly lost it again. He kissed her. And she made the same humming sound of appreciation she made at the dinner table. He felt like every bit of control was being eaten away by her responses. What was it about this woman?

He began to move slowly at first, then more quickly. When she gave herself over to his rhythm, her body gripping and releasing him, he was lost. His orgasm struck with an intensity that went on and on and on.

Beneath him, Moira panted just as hard as he was, her breasts heaving against him. One arm slipped upward to curve around his neck, and she tucked her lips against his throat as her other hand followed the line of his spine down, then back up again.

Because he wanted to stay inside her for at least the next millennium, he forced himself to withdraw and rolled onto his side next to her.

She curled on her side facing him, her blue-green gaze drowsy with release.

"Going to stay?"

Sleeping with someone was more intimate than making love, and he avoided it most of the time. But faced with the vulnerable look in her eyes while she invited him to stay, he couldn't say no. If he did, it would put what they'd just done in the light of a booty call, and she deserved better than that. "I'll have to leave early. I want to check on one of my men at the hospital before reporting to base."

"Book?"

"Yeah."

She stroked his cheek.

That tender touch seemed to reach right down into his gut. "I need to deal with things. I'll be right back." He rolled out of bed and wandered into the bathroom. When he returned, she'd pulled down the bedclothes and comforter and was wearing a long, paint-splattered, oversized T-shirt that hung to the middle of her thighs. She combed her fingers through the wild curls that rested over one shoulder. He'd never seen anything sexier.

She took off her glasses and placed them on the nightstand, and he recognized the vulnerability in the gesture. The glasses acted as a window or a barrier and a clue to her emotions. For her to shed them was another indication that she'd lowered more barriers.

Dammit!

There was an awkward moment when they both climbed into bed from opposite sides. Moira turned her back and pulled the covers up over her shoulder. Sam reached for the lights and turned them off.

A long moment of silence followed where he tried hard not to reach for her. He wasn't the cuddling kind. He needed his own space. She was giving it to him...wasn't she? Dammit!

Fuck it! He scooted closer and snuggled her back against him to spoon, and knew, when she rested a hand over his against her midsection, he'd done the right thing. He was asleep in minutes.

CHAPTER 4

THE SOUND OF someone moving around the room penetrated Moira's sleep-dulled mind, and she squinted against the hazy glow of a light outside shining through the balcony blinds. "What time is it?" she asked, her voice husky with sleep.

Sam walked past her, though she couldn't see anything but his dark shape, and couldn't see his face. "It's four hundred hours. Go back to sleep." He bent and kissed her forehead, then her lips. "We'll talk later."

He'd woken her sometime during the night, his hands on her breasts, his teeth nibbling her earlobe, and she'd been lost once again in a sexual haze of need.

She'd never known anything like it. All she had to do was think about what they'd done for her body to quicken again.

A few minutes later the door opened, flooding the carpet with a narrow rectangle of light that was cut off when he shut it behind him.

Moira rolled onto her back, yawned and stretched. Would he really call her, or would she just be a random lay, a one-night stand? She hoped he thought more of her than that.

But she wasn't going to waste her time with regret, especially after having five orgasms in one night. Hadn't really believed she'd ever know what even one orgasm was like. And now she did... Now she knew what she'd been missing, she was glad she waited.

She wasn't a pity fuck this time. Sam wanted her. Really wanted her. Would she be able to put those painful moments behind her now?

She threw back the covers and rose to go into the bathroom. She was a little tender in spots she never had been before, and a little sleep-deprived, but other than that she felt terrific.

On her way out of the bathroom, she wiggled into her sleep shirt, grabbed her windbreaker and put it on, retrieved her glasses from the nightstand, unlocked the balcony door, and stepped out. Taking a deep breath of the fresh, chilly air, she snuggled the windbreaker more tightly around her.

She took in the pale blue of the ocean and the distant haze over the businesses east across the bay. Took the time to really study the Hotel Del, which was more like a miniature city with its towers and cabanas, restaurants, swimming pools, spa, clothing boutiques, and other amenities. She spied a couple of people wandering about the grounds, probably employees.

Resting her arms atop the railing and leaning forward to look down, she noticed a scrap of white on the ground beneath one of the bushes. Had someone dropped a towel?

Her attention kept returning to that scrap of white deep in the shadows, and just below the boughs of the hedge…was that a man's shoe and his pants leg?

The more she stared at it, the more she was convinced that's what it was. Someone might have fainted or fallen. She returned to her room and slipped on the pants and blouse from the night before and put her windbreaker back on. Finding the elevator, she went to the ground floor and out a side door.

The structure, rambling and huge, once again reminded her of the decks of a cruise ship. Reaching the sidewalk, she followed it to the side of the building facing the ocean, and crossed the grass, looking up at the second-floor balconies to locate her room.

The man's leather dress shoes shone dully in the glow of a nearby light. He was slumped against the side of the building, his feet straight out in front of him, the satin strip of a tuxedo pants leg leading back to the man himself. Maybe he just had too much to drink.

Moira took out her phone and used the screen to light the man's face, and the glow captured the threads of silver in Mark Travis's hair and the glassy glint of dead eyes fixed in a dull stare. Blood darkened his temple, the shoulder of his suit and his shirt, but it was the odd angle at which his head rested that had set off nausea strong enough to make her gag.

The moment he shook her hand ran through her mind. She turned away to keep from throwing up on the body, but managed to regain control—barely. Her hands shook as she dialed nine-one-one.

Even though the dispatch officer asking her questions distracted her, she moved away from the body and sat on the ground. It seemed to take forever for the police to arrive, but finally the sound of a siren carried on the wind, faint at first, like the buzzing of a fly, then rising to a scream.

She scrambled to her feet and braced herself to meet them. Against her will, her eyes kept straying back to Mark Travis's body and the concave spot in the ground about two feet to the left of it. She looked up at the balconies above. He might have fallen from one of them. But when?

SAM TURNED AWAY from the window and his study of the parking lots, buildings, and streets that stretched away from Balboa Military Hospital, and wandered back to the chair next to Book's hospital bed. Monitors attached to the SEAL's body tracked his heart rate, blood pressure, and oxygen levels.

The hospital was more peaceful early in the morning, and it was easier for him to visit before reporting for duty. The nurses didn't seem to mind, even though it wasn't visiting hours.

How could a guy go through three tours without a scratch and almost get killed on a training exercise? He wondered about Alisha, Book's fianceé. Swan had been so adamant that Book was making a mistake.

Alisha had seemed beyond upset when she first saw Elijah, who'd been unconscious, his body one huge bruise and his leg in a plaster cast to his hip. Her concern had seemed genuine.

The docs weren't sure yet whether he'd lost enough blood to have starved his brain of oxygen. If that was the case…he'd be a vegetable. How would she handle that?

Sam ran a hand over his hair and fought off the feeling of helplessness. He was used to working the problem, making sure he and his men survived no matter what they had to do. But he couldn't do a damn thing but wait and see what fate had in store for Book. As bad as he looked, Book had come through impossible situations in combat. He was strong, focused and determined. Sam wasn't giving up on him yet.

"I met a woman last night," he said, though he didn't think Book could hear him. "She's beautiful and smart. An art teacher. So, she's probably talented too. I told her things about my family I haven't talked about in a long time. Probably shouldn't have done that, but she was easy to talk to. She has this peacefulness about her. She pays attention to what you say, I mean real attention, like she's listening for the undercurrents in your voice or something."

Book's face remained passive.

"The team's being put in charge of the seven-week phase of a BUD/S class while they finish with their investigation into your accident. Seems strange to be moving on as though nothing happened while you're in here, Book. You need to get your ass in gear and heal up. Get back to your team. We need you.

"Also, they've suspended jumps until they're certain no other parachutes are compromised.

Sam ran a hand over his jaw, beard stubble rough against his palm. "What's going on with Swan, Book? Did he lie to me when he said he'd never dated Alisha? Or is that why he was so adamant about you calling off the wedding? And why he's acting so damn guilty now?"

Maybe Sam would have some answers by the time Book woke up. Until they brought the kid out of his coma, they wouldn't know about his cognitive abilities, and doing it right now would wake him to a living hell of pain. His injuries were so extensive it would be inhumane.

But this waiting game was a bitch.

Sam rose and paced back to the window to look out over the parking area below. He only had forty-five minutes before he had to report to base. Time to get a move on.

He turned and his attention snagged on a card resting on the laminated top of the nightstand. He strode over and picked it up. The outside was just a picture of the ocean. Inside two words were written. *I'm sorry.*

CHAPTER 5

"HOW DID YOU find the body?" Broad and burly, Detective Buckler had the look of a serious weightlifter and could probably bench press a truck. His partner, Detective Hart, had the lanky frame of a runner, round chin, and dark, intense eyes. Both had the worn, lived-in faces of cops who had gone around the block several times and seen things other people wouldn't want to.

Moira drew her windbreaker around her, still feeling chilled despite the hot cup of tea one of the staff brought her to settle her stomach. The small sitting area the detectives directed her to was quiet and out of the way enough that what they discussed couldn't be overheard.

"I was standing out on the balcony of my room, resting my arms on the railing. When I looked down, I saw something white. At first I thought it was a towel. But fairly close to it was what looked like a man's shoe. Because of my glasses I thought it could be a trick of the light. You can imagine you see so many things in shadows, and the overhang of the upper balcony and railing kept it dark there. Then I thought maybe someone had too much to drink and passed out, or might have fallen. Either way I decided to go down and see if someone needed help."

"Did you know the deceased?" Detective Hart asked.

"No. I only met him last night and spoke just long enough to say 'nice to meet you.' Mrs. Travis was getting ready to give out the awards at the banquet, and I needed to get back to my table. But I did see him outside after the banquet, a little after eleven."

"Was he with anyone?"

"A woman." She looked down into her cup. "Not his wife." She took a tentative sip of the tea and set it aside. "They were in a passionate embrace so I couldn't see her face, but she was dressed formally like she'd attended the banquet. Her dress was crimson, and her hair dark. I believe she was young, since her skin was smooth and her fingernails were painted to match the dress. She was several inches shorter than he was, because his shoulder kept me from being able to see much of her."

"What were you doing outside?"

"I met a man at dinner, and we talked all through our meal. After we left the banquet, we took a walk on the beach, and saw them before we reached the sand. We were gone about an hour, maybe a little more."

"What's this man's name?"

"Sam Harding. He's a lieutenant in the Navy. His father and brothers practice law here in San Diego. They were out of town, and his mother urged him to attend the banquet to represent the family. He had to report to the base a little after five this morning."

"About what time was it last night when you saw Mark Travis on the sidewalk outside the side entrance?"

"A little after eleven."

"How far down the sidewalk were they?"

"It was just outside the side door at the corner of the building."

"Do you have Harding's contact information? We'd like to speak to him."

"I have his phone number." She pulled her phone free of her jacket pocket, scrolled through for the text, and handed it to Detective Buckler.

"Have you stayed here before, Ms. McKee?" Detective Hart asked.

"No. It's a little out of my price range. But I've always been interested in the historic part of the hotel. When my school received an invitation to send a representative to attend, and my principal asked me to do it, I made a reservation. That was two months ago. I took a personal day off today so I could explore the grounds a little and take some pictures before I check out. I'm an artist and a teacher. I'm always looking for interesting venues to paint. And to challenge my students to draw." She gazed around the lobby with its richly paneled walls gleaming with care, the staircase, the elaborate brass elevator and the soaring, vaulted ceiling with its patterned beams.

"Don't let this experience ruin your stay here. It's usually a safe, family place."

"Thank you." She debated with herself about whether to repeat what Sam told her about Mark. When the two detectives rose, she let it pass.

"Try and put this behind you and enjoy the rest of your stay, Ms. McKee," Detective Buckler urged.

"You're not concerned it was a mugger on the hotel grounds?"

"It's too early to say, but I believe you'll be safe to take your pictures. And we'll have a police presence on the grounds."

They didn't think Travis's death was random. Perhaps his lifestyle had finally caught up with him.

"We'd like to check out the view from your room if you wouldn't mind."

"I don't mind." They took the elevator upstairs.

"How long have you been teaching?"

"This is my sixth year. I've really enjoyed it this year. I have a great group of kids."

She unlocked the door and stepped aside to let them in. Both detectives walked past the tumbled bed without comment, though her cheeks flushed hot when she saw the rumpled sheets. They'd know she spent the night with someone.

Through the balcony door she watched the detectives walk up and down the balcony, checking the railing. Then one peered over it.

She scanned the room. Her evening gown visible inside the open closet. Her suitcase lay open on the luggage rack. The bed was a wreck, so she smoothed the covers. Getting out fresh panties and a bra, she took them and her cosmetic bag into the bathroom. After the detectives left she'd have a shower, take her photos, then go home to paint and try to get her mind off of Mark Travis's glazed eyes and bulging neck.

By now they had told Elizabeth Travis her husband was dead. Told her son. Life would never be the same for either of them. The argument between father and son during dinner came to mind. Typical teenage behavior. She hoped it wasn't the last thing he said to his father.

Had Elizabeth looked for her husband last night? Called around to try and find him?

She rubbed her arms, though she still wore the windbreaker.

Detective Hart broke into her thoughts as he came in from the balcony and scanned the room.

"You're sure you didn't know the victim?"

"No. Like I said, I only met him for about thirty seconds."

"Did Lieutenant Harding spend the night here with you?"

Her face felt hot and she moistened her lips. Forced herself to meet his gaze. "Yes, he did."

His expression remained bland. He handed her a card. "If you think of anything else you haven't told us, just call."

"I will." She followed the two detectives to the door, then shut and locked it. She moved to the balcony door and tried it, and finding it locked, pulled the drapes.

She didn't want to worry about what the detectives thought of her behavior. And if Sam didn't call later like he said he would....

He knew the people involved, and he'd been at the dinner. They'd call him, and he'd admit to being with her, and that would be the end of it. The detectives didn't know her or him. They probably didn't think a thing about two single people hooking up.

She glanced at her watch. He'd already be on the base. She'd call him later.

She and Sam would go sailing on Sunday, get to know each

other a little better without the sex. And who knows? They might decide they had more things in common. She needed to relax and let nature take its course.

She'd already learned to enjoy making love with him. Maybe she'd learn what it was like to actually have a real relationship with a man.

Somehow she'd never believed she'd get to this point. Going after something she wanted for herself was foreign to her. Well, something professional, sure, but not personal. And there wasn't anything more personal than letting a man see you naked and…he hadn't noticed the stretch marks on her breasts and hips. Or if he had, it didn't seem to affect the way he looked at her.

She hoped he called.

SWEAT RAN IN rivulets between Sam's shoulder blades, soaking his T-shirt. The night's wind had dissipated, leaving behind calm, and without the breeze the sun felt like a blowtorch aimed at the top of his head. Dragging a sweat-stained baseball cap out of his back pocket, he pulled it on, then added his sunglasses. His team were all there to instruct and harass the next round of BUD/S candidates, to see what they were made of first, then to weed out the ones who didn't have the temperament or stamina to stick it out. After that they'd whip them into the toughest damn fighting machines in the world.

Even though he wasn't participating in the physical labor of picking up the hundred-and-fifty-pound log and holding it over his head, he understood the men's pain. It was during Log PT that the men either learned to work together or their eight-man team would fall apart and more would ring that bell in the quad.

His cell phone buzzed against his hip and he glanced at the screen. The number was on post, so he brushed the screen to unlock it and answered the call.

"Lieutenant Harding, this is Ensign Elliot, Captain DeLano's Adjutant."

He'd have recognized Elliot's Brooklyn accent even if he hadn't identified himself. "Yes, Ensign. What can I do for you?"

"There are two police officers here at the office who want to talk to you."

Police? Had something happened to his father and brothers? His stomach tightened. "What is it they want to talk to me about, Ensign?"

"It seems one of the guests at a function you attended last night was killed and they're touching base with everyone who was there."

A guest was killed? Before he could ask who, the Ensign rushed on.

"Captain DeLano has ordered your relief so you can take care of this. He's sending transport to drop Lieutenant O'Connor off and pick you up. Where is your current location?"

"We're on the beach conducting Log PT, Ensign."

"I'm sending them now."

"Roger that."

Who the hell was dead? And when did it happen?

It had to have happened at the Del if they were interviewing everyone who attended the fundraiser last night.

Concern ricocheted through him. He left Moira safe in bed. But she'd been planning to go swimming. He punched Moira's number in his contacts. The call went to voicemail and he swore.

A jeep appeared in the distance. He pocketed his phone and called Squirrel over. "I have to go up to Captain DeLano's office and meet with some people. Lieutenant O'Connor will be relieving me."

Squirrel gave him a thumb's up. "Roger that, LT."

Sam pushed the concerned tension back and fought the urge to try Moira again.

The jeep kicked up sand as it came to a halt and Lieutenant Zach O'Connor swung out of the vehicle, his red hair aflame in the afternoon sun. Sam met him halfway with a handshake. "Thanks for covering for me. I'll be back as soon as I can."

"No problem."

"How'd the wedding go?" Sam had been invited to Zach and Piper's nuptials, but had been out of the country.

"With her Catholic family and mine combined, it was huge. And she didn't bail." Zach held up his left hand showing off a shiny gold band.

Sam laughed. "I didn't think she would. Sorry I missed it." The two seemed a good match. Piper was in partnership with several other vets at a thriving office, and stayed as busy as Zach. "I owe you a bottle of wine."

"Come to the next barbecue and bring some beer, and we'll call it even."

"I'm up for that." Sam threw up a hand and hauled ass to the jeep.

Reaching the brick building that housed Captain DeLano's office, he hit the head, splashed water on his face to cool off, and washed his hands. And realized he was stalling while he prepared himself for whatever the detectives had to say. If it was Moira....

Ensign Elliot rose from his desk and handed him a bottle of water. "Thought you might need something to drink after coming off the beach, sir," his Brooklyn accent was thick.

"Yeah, I do. Thanks, Ensign."

"You're welcome, sir. I've put them in one of our smaller meeting rooms. Second door down."

Sam nodded and wandered back out of the office and down the hall, where he opened the door and stepped in. The two detectives stood and exchanged quick introductions and handshakes with him. They looked a little worn around the edges.

"We appreciate you coming in out of the field to speak to us."

"No problem." He wasn't waiting any longer. "I met a woman last night, ate dinner at her table, shared a few dances with her and a walk on the beach. She was planning to go swimming this morning. Her name is Moira McKee. You're not here about her, are you?"

"No, Lieutenant."

The tension in his shoulders and back released. "Who was killed?"

"Mark Travis."

His dispassionate feelings at hearing that bit of news kept him from reacting.

"You haven't heard any news reports this morning?"

"No. I've been on the beach all morning doing PT with BUD/S candidates."

"Did you know Mark Travis?" Detective Hart asked.

"Only slightly. He's a member of the country club where my father and stepmother golf. I think my father has golfed with him a time or two. I don't travel in the same crowd as my father and his wife."

"You saw Travis last night, though."

"Yes, but we never spoke." He'd been struck down with tunnel vision from the moment he saw Moira. Something he'd never experienced before. "Moira and I didn't speak to him outside the hotel either. We walked right by him while he was kissing a woman who wasn't Elizabeth, and with both hands clamped on her ass."

"You weren't surprised?"

"Surprised to come upon a couple kissing in a public place, yes. Shocked that it was Mark Travis, no. He has—had—a reputation for sleeping around on his wife. And he didn't worry about being seen with other women." Other people they interviewed today were bound to say the same thing.

"How do you know this wasn't his wife?"

"Mrs. Travis had on a pale peach gown. She was on the stage several times, so it was easy to remember. I got the impression this woman was younger, had narrower hips, was thinner.

"I didn't see her face, but her dress was dark red, made of some kind of shiny fabric, and she was short, almost tiny. They had photographers recording the event, so they probably photographed her if she attended the banquet."

"You didn't notice her there?"

"No. I was focused on the other people at my table, and later, on dancing with Ms. McKee."

"What time did you leave the hotel?"

He hesitated. He didn't want to embarrass Moira, but he couldn't hold back or the two would think he was hiding something related to the murder. "I left Moira about four this morning. I had to go by the hospital and check on an injured teammate, then had to be on post by oh-five-hundred to rouse the candidates."

The two detectives stood. Sam did as well. Detective Buckler handed him a card. "If you think of anything that might be helpful, give us a call."

"Roger that, Detective."

As soon as they were gone, Sam pulled out his phone to call Moira again.

"Hello."

That one word relieved his tension. "The police were just here to interview me. Are you okay?"

"Yes, I'm on my way home. I was the one who found the body, Sam."

"Jesus! Are you sure you're all right?"

"Yeah, still a little shaky, and every time I think about it, I get sick to my stomach."

"I'd come hang with you for the day if I didn't have to work, Moira."

"Thanks."

His dick hardened at the soft sound of her voice.

"Would you like to come to dinner tonight?" she asked.

"What time?"

"How's six-thirty?"

"I'll be there."

"You have my address."

"I have it in my phone."

"Okay, I'll see you then."

When he closed out the call, he stared at the phone. Jesus, she found Mark Travis's dead body. But when and how?

On his way back to the beach he spotted Swan as he jogged toward one of the equipment buildings on the Silver Strand. "You can let me out, Seaman Crest. I'll jog back from here. Go on down to the beach and pick up Lieutenant O'Connor."

"Yes, sir." The young seaman pulled the jeep over and Sam leapt out, taking up a position outside the door Swan had entered. This was as good a time as any to get this behind them both.

The door flew open ten minutes later, and Swan pulled up, his expression one of surprise. "Looking for me, LT?"

"Yeah, we need to talk. Come on, we'll walk while we do it."

"What's going on?" Swan asked, dodging around one of the shrubs planted along the sidewalk.

"I want to know why you were on Book's ass about marrying Alisha."

Swan's expression hardened. "He'd regret it later. Women are all bad news."

Swan had been singing that tune for as long as Sam had known him. "All women? Or just Alisha? Did you date her before Book did?"

"Yes, all women, and no, I've never dated her, but I know she was a stripper for a while at a club some of the guys used to go to."

"What club?"

"The Honey Pot. It's closed down now. The owner was killed by one of his girls. News was he was molesting the girls and blackballing them from working at other clubs to keep them from quitting."

"And that would be Alisha's fault because...?"

"It wasn't her fault. But Book is one of the good guys, and he doesn't need to hook up with a stripper. I mean...Jesus!"

Shit! He had to have first-hand knowledge. "You went there, didn't you?"

"Well, yeah."

"Did she give you a lap dance?"

Swan's mouth twisted into a snarl. "No, but she did one of the guys on another team while I was there. There's no telling how many she's rubbed around on. It'd be common knowledge around the base eventually, and Book would pay for that."

"You're talking about him in the past tense, as though he's

dead."

"The chances he'll come back from the…accident…are slim, LT"

"He hasn't given up yet, Swan, and I'm not giving up on him. We're going to be there for him as a team. If you don't want any part of that, you might want to put in for a transfer."

Swan was silent for a long moment. "I don't want a transfer."

If Swan had something to do with Book's chute, would he jump at the chance to transfer out? Or was everything just bad luck? Sam wouldn't know until results from the investigation came through. They came out over the scrub onto the rolling dunes that led down onto the beach.

"Do you want me to put in for one?" Swan asked, his expression sullen.

Better to have him where he could keep an eye on him. "No. Did you leave a card on Book's bedside table?"

"No. I've only been to see him once for about fifteen minutes. His sister was there, and I didn't see any cards."

"Okay." The cerulean blue water created a backdrop for the sand-caked teams of men jogging up and down the beach holding logs over their heads.

"Is Book awake?" Swan asked.

"No. They're purposely keeping him in a coma and waiting until his injuries have healed some before they wake him." He homed in on Swan's face. "He may not walk again."

Swan flinched. "Jesus." His throat worked and his hands balled into fists. "Do the others know?"

"No. Not yet. I'll tell them when we send the class in for chow."

Swan nodded. "It's going to hit them hard, LT. He's like our little brother."

"Yeah, he is. And a damn good SEAL. Whatever it takes, he'll get out of that bed and move on with his life." Sam hoped it would be true.

Swan bobbed his head one last time and jogged down the beach to join the other instructors in berating and encouraging the men.

Sam followed at a slower pace. As obsessed as Swan was about saving Book from the evils of hooking up with the wrong woman, he couldn't see him purposely killing Book to save him. And the way he talked about Alishia being a stripper....

But then he didn't know the woman, or how deep into the stripping life she'd been. Not all of them prostituted themselves.

Had she been one of the girls abused by their boss? Was Book marrying her out of some kind of overactive protective urge?

It didn't really matter right now why the kid was getting married. The wedding would be postponed. And he'd first need to concentrate on surviving.

But who the hell had left the card? The printing on the message had been blocky and succinct, more male than female. And why just the words "I'm sorry"?

Like Swan said, they all thought of him as a little brother.

Which only made things more difficult. For everyone.

CHAPTER 6

MOIRA UNPACKED FROM her overnight stay, changed into her normal weekend uniform of leggings and a long top, and settled at her workstation in the bedroom to download her photos of the Hotel Del.

The light had been a little harsh even at seven in the morning, but she'd captured some beautiful exterior shots of the hotel, the beach and surf, the lounges and umbrellas, some of the grounds. The interior photos of the lobby were a little dark. She adjusted the light, brightening them and enhancing the golden glow of the wood under the light of the chandeliers.

Next she deepened the contrast on some of the exterior shots, and printed them all out. She'd use them in her advanced drawing class.

Then she pulled out the photos she'd taken of the hotel balconies and studied them.

She'd overheard some of the staff saying it was likely Mark Travis had fallen off of one of the balconies or been pushed. The odd concave depression close to his body aligned with that supposition. Since he was lying just below her room, he either fell from the floor above, or someone had moved the body after he fell. He'd have no reason to be on her balcony.

And she hadn't heard a fight, or even the sound of him falling during the night. But she and Sam were a little distracted at the time.

She wondered about the girl Travis was kissing. She shook her head. Poor Elizabeth. Every secret he ever kept would come to light because of the way he died.

Elizabeth Travis had lost a child and now her husband. Those alone would be extremely painful, but now she'd have to live through every indiscretion he ever committed. And it would probably impact the charity.

Moira had to do something to get this off her mind, and shake the memory of Travis's glazed, dead eyes and—God, his neck!

She needed to work. She stacked the printed photos, put them in a folder. She approached her current work in progress on her easel. She had a few photographs of the woman, but this one was inspired by her client's dream. She'd done preliminary drawings from the man's descriptions and then worked with him closely for more than two hours.

She squeezed alizarin crimson, yellow ochre, Phthalo blue, and several other colors onto her pallette and went to work, losing herself in the painting, in the process of applying the paint, mixing and blending colors, creating the vision her client had described. The woman's figure took shape, misty yet haunting.

For the face she had a photo of the man's wife. She pulled it out of the folder.

The woman's features were delicate, but there was strength in her jaw, and her eyes, an intense blue, sparkled with humor and intelligence.

Moira did a practice drawing in pastel before transferring it to the canvas, then took a break to get something to drink and to bundle her hair into a topknot, sticking two paintbrushes into the mass to hold it in place.

She lost herself in the struggle to get the features right, the color, to bring the focal point of the dream, the woman, to life. She put the finishing touches on the face then looked up at the sound of her apartment intercom going off.

Sam. "Oh, shit!" She looked at her paint-covered hands and the pallette she hadn't cleaned, and ran for the door. She pushed the intercom button. "Sam?"

"Yeah."

"Come on up. Apartment two-oh-eight." Lord she'd promised to fix a meal. Did she even have anything on hand to cook? She forced herself to pause and relax a moment. If she didn't have anything, they'd go out and she'd treat him to a meal. It would be just fine.

But now that she thought about it, she was starving. *Chicken!* She had chicken and all sorts of vegetables.

She rushed into the kitchen to clean up and noticed a streak of blue along one arm. She wiped at it with a damp paper towel and went to answer the door.

After he left her at the Del, she thought her imagination might have exaggerated how compellingly sexy he was—until she opened the door.

His smile hit her libido, sending tingles out to every sensitive area of her body. No, no exaggeration there. His warm brown eyes, like dark toffee, raked downward, taking in her leggings and the slouchy shirt hanging off one shoulder. "Come on in. I've been working and lost track of time."

She'd seen him in formal wear and his camouflage uniform. Now he was wearing jeans, well-worn and clean, and a white cotton shirt with the sleeves rolled back to bare muscular forearms.

"Grading papers?" he asked as he stepped into the living room.

"No, I paint on commission, and I've almost finished my current project. I need to clean up a little before starting dinner." She scanned the living area, looking for anything untidy she could whisk away. The neutral couch and chairs acted as the anchor for the bold, bright blues, reds, purples, and yellows of the paintings on the walls, and textured pillows were piled on either end of the couch. A braided area rug of cream and brown warmed the dark tile floor that ran throughout the apartment, a cream, tan, and black afghan draped across the back of a chair, and a peacock blue scarf spread on her coffee table hung off two sides in triangular points. And in the center sat a hand-thrown pottery dish holding a large candle surrounded by glass crystals that reflected the pops of color all around the room.

The dining area was small and just off the kitchen. A smaller braided rug just like the one in the living area lay beneath an oval dining table with a large, flower-shaped ceramic bowl of fresh fruit.

"This space suits you. It's both colorful and restful."

"Thanks. My studio space is down here. It'll just take a few minutes to clean up."

She entered her work room which, unlike the rest of the apartment, was barren of both a rug and curtains. A storage cabinet stood in one corner holding spare stretched canvases, and in another a computer desk with a laptop, printer, and attached filing cabinet. Near the window stood a table littered with her palette, tubes of paint, palette knives, brushes, cloths, and cups of water. She unclamped the wax paper she'd used to cover the palette, wadded it up, and dropped it into the trash can, then put her used brushes into a container partially filled with water and picked up both it and a container of muddy water she'd rinsed her brushes in as she worked.

Sam moved to stand before the twenty-four by thirty-six canvas locked onto her easel and studied it. "This is amazing, Moira."

"It's an image from my client's dream. The woman is his wife." She studied the portrait with a critical eye. Done in washes of pastel blues and grays, the woman's figure was clothed in a thin, wispy, scarf-like bathing suit cover plastered to her body by a wind that seemed to mold and caress her. The fabric allowed her lightly tanned skin to glow. The afternoon sun touched the bright hazelnut highlights in her hair, and she walked on a beach of pale gold. The ocean behind her was dark and choppy, whitecaps frothing on its surface. The way the man talked about his wife had touched her deeply, and she was pleased that his passion for his wife found its way onto the canvas.

"There's something sexy as hell about this."

"That's what the client wanted. It's for their sixth wedding anniversary."

He looked over his shoulder at her with a grin. "He's so going to get laid."

She laughed. "Probably. Women like romantic gestures. Especially when it's a surprise."

He raised a brow. "I'll keep that in mind."

He was so good at flirting. Dressed in jeans and the white shirt that strained across his wide shoulders and powerful chest, he looked as though he probably got plenty of practice.

And practice made perfect. She already knew he was as practiced at other things. Her cheeks flushed hot. What made him home in on her? Had she come across as the gullible, inexperienced fool she was?

She swallowed and tried to keep her sudden nerves out of her voice. "Beer or wine? I think I'm doing stir fry."

He grinned. "Wine."

"Wine it is." She turned and led the way to the kitchen, where she emptied the water containers and ran some water in one side of the double sink for her brushes to soak.

She opened the refrigerator to study the shelves.

Sam leaned against the kitchen Island. "Can I do anything to help?"

"We're having chicken, since I have some. You can choose a wine for that. The wine fridge is over there." She pointed a stalk of celery toward the small dining table and the wine fridge next to it. "The corkscrew is in the bowl on the kitchen table."

"We could go out."

"I'm prone to getting lost in my work and forgetting until I'm half starved. And I am, since I didn't feel like eating earlier in the day. I don't mind cooking, and it'll take less time for me to cook than for us to decide where to go."

SAM WATCHED HER quick, economical movements as she set water on the stove to boil and measured out two cups of rice in a large measuring cup. She cut up chicken and tossed it into a pan to sear.

"What have you been up to today?" she asked.

SEAL training wasn't a secret. It had been filmed, photographed, and had books written about it, so he relaxed into the telling. "We spent the morning and afternoon on the beach doing PT. A lot of what we do builds stamina and strength, but the intent of a lot of the things we do is to help the guys learn to work together as a team."

While he told her about some of the exercises, she flipped the slivers of chicken and splashed a little soy sauce over them, then poured the rice into the boiling water, stirred it, turned down the heat to a soft boil, and put a lid on the pot. He offered her the wine glass.

"Thanks." She took a sip and closed her eyes to savor it before setting the glass aside. She dragged out a chopping board and started slicing and dicing.

Sam moved to stand where she could glance up at him as they talked.

She carried the chopping board to the stove to toss a handful of this and that in the skillet, as though she were mixing colors for a composition, little red pepper here, slices of yellow and zucchini squash, slivers of carrot, onions, celery, large florets of broccoli, a heaping handful of sliced mushrooms, over which she poured in a concoction of honey, garlic, ginger, cornstarch and broth. "That has to cook for five minutes for the sauce to thicken." She set the timer and turned the heat under the rice off.

She leaned back against the counter. "You got some sun today. As attractive as a tan is, you need to wear sunscreen."

"Normally I do. Somewhere between the office and the beach I lost my hat, and then I got busy and forgot. When you're in the middle of…things…sunscreen is a low priority."

She set aside her wine glass and stepped over to the cabinet at the corner, reached inside to get a tube of something, and sauntered back again. "This is aloe, and it'll soothe the burn."

She gently brushed the gel over first one cheekbone, then the other. The dry burn eased immediately.

"Better?" Her blue-green eyes held a look in their depths that had him reaching for her. He rested his hands on her hips as the same meteoric desire he experienced the first time they met swamped him. His heart pounded like a drum and his dick hardened.

"Yeah, thanks." He bent his head to brush a kiss against her bare shoulder and felt her shiver.

Color bloomed in her cheeks, and she turned her mouth to meet his. She tasted of wine and her. In the thin leggings and top she felt almost naked as he brought her flush against him. As her tongue met and mated with his in a tempting dance, he wanted to sink to the floor where they stood and bury himself inside her. He molded her against him, his hands restless and hungry for the feel of her.

The timer buzzed and they both groaned.

She pulled away from him to turn off the heat beneath the skillet and stir its contents. She turned to face him. "After you left this morning...I wondered if you'd call. I mean...

"I actually planned to call at lunch while the guys ate, but the detectives showed up at the base and I was called to the office for an interview."

The tension in her features relaxed. "You're only the second man I've been with."

He'd known she wasn't very experienced. She been shy about touching him and had seemed all instinct. She'd been so responsive...but he hadn't expected... His dick was hard as stone, and he barely managed to hear her voice through a haze of blood drumming in his ears.

"There are things you need to know about me, and there are things I want to know about you." She got plates and silverware out and pushed them into his hands. "Please set the table."

Her controlled reasonable tone, her schoolteacher syntax, pierced his hard-on haze, and the breathless tremor in her voice made him smile. And he was struck once again by a protective rush of emotion.

How the hell was he supposed to protect her when he was the one who wanted her naked?

He found napkins on top of the wine fridge and set the table.

She carried two bowls to the table, one of rice and the other of the meat and vegetables.

Her cheeks were still a little flushed when she came back to the table. He held her chair for her.

"I'll get the wine and our glasses." By the time he returned to the table her color was closer to normal.

He poured more wine while she scooped rice and stir-fry onto her plate.

"This looks great." He dug into the bowls and filled his own.

She took a bite of broccoli. "I took some wonderful photos of the hotel, the beach, and the grounds this morning. I'll show them to you after we eat, if you're interested."

"Sure. I'm as bad at photography as I'd be at painting, but I enjoy seeing what other people can do with it." He shoveled in a bite of the stir fry to find it was damn good. The vegetables were still crisp, the sauce both tangy and sweet.

"I could teach you to paint as easily as you taught me to dance."

It was true she'd only stepped on his toes once, but she wasn't even close to being proficient. "You've only had one lesson. You could probably use a few more."

She chuckled. "You have a much more diplomatic way with words than my brothers." She nibbled a piece of chicken.

"What would your brothers say?"

"That I really suck and it's a damn miracle you weren't crippled."

He laughed. "Are they older or younger?"

"Both. I'm the middle child with two on one side and two on the other. The youngest, Kyle, who's 14, was a surprise to us all."

"I just have the two brothers, Trevor and Timothy. Both are in business with my father. I'm the oldest." He took a sip of wine.

"And your mother?" she urged.

"She's a cardiac nurse at Balboa."

"Wow, brave lady. My mother's a college professor, history."

"Where does she teach?"

"University of California Berkley."

"No, shit. I went to UC Berkley. Ms. McKee." He thought about it trying to bring up a face. "Sandy blonde hair with a little gray at the temples, and your eyes."

"Yeah. Did you take her class?"

"No, but I've met her. Small world."

"I'll have to ask her if she remembers you."

"Out of hundreds of students? And I didn't even have her in class."

"She's spooky that way. Laser vision." She laughed.

"Did you go to UC?"

"No. I went to UCLA to get a degree in Art Education. I got a scholarship."

"I can see why."

"Actually, it wasn't for my artistic skills, but for academics. The number of people who are able to make a living selling their art are few and far between. I got the education degree as a backup and do the artwork on the side."

He wiped his mouth with a napkin. "I think you're good enough to make a living at it. I'm obviously not an art expert, but that painting you're doing is damn amazing."

"Thanks." The way she said it held a hint of embarrassment.

"What does your dad do?"

"He's a pharmacist at one of the large chains. My two oldest brothers, Devin and Dustin, are architects, and both work for the same firm. The one two years younger than me, Mitchell, followed in dad's footsteps and is a pharmacist."

"And the youngest one is playing shortstop."

"Yes." She smiled. "Kyle's a good kid. He's had all six of us riding herd on him since birth, so he doesn't stand a chance of being anything else."

Sam laughed. "We only had Mom from the time I was fourteen, but actually even before. She did a fine job despite the demands of her work." While his dad had been diddling his new side piece. How many other women had there been before he learned about Delia, the woman his father had been seeing and then later married?

The bastard probably still had a side piece even now.

She placed a hand on his arm, and he focused in on her. There was something comforting in her demeanor. "I have some frozen yogurt if you'd like dessert. I don't really keep sweets in the house."

"Thanks, but no. I'm full. It was good. You can cook."

"Do you cook?"

"I can if I'm hungry enough."

She laughed. "That's what my brothers say."

"I can fix breakfast. Grill any kind of meat, and nuke vegetables in the microwave. That's all the skills a guy needs to survive."

She shook her head and rose to clear the table. He grabbed his plate and the rice bowl before she could touch them and followed her into the kitchen. "You cooked. I can do the dishes."

"I'm going to rinse everything and put them in the dishwasher later." She pulled out plastic wrap, covered the bowls and stuck them in the refrigerator, then stacked the plates in the sink. "Let's take our wine out on the balcony and talk."

They settled on the pocket-sized balcony in cushioned lawn chairs, a small table between them.

"How is your teammate?" she asked.

"He's in a medically induced coma until his body heals enough for him to bear the pain."

"God, I'm so sorry."

At the empathy in her tone, he brushed the backs of his fingers against her cheek and was rewarded by another of those looks that set off his libido. He leaned forward in his chair and held the wine glass between his fingertips. "Do you want to talk about what happened today?"

"I suppose if I don't talk about it I'll probably have nightmares."

She'd probably have nightmares even if she did. "How did you end up finding Mark Travis?"

"After you left, I couldn't go back to sleep. So I decided to get up and go out on the balcony to look out over the grounds. While I was leaning on the railing and looking down, I noticed something white below. I thought it was a towel, but then I noticed a shape in the shadows that looked like a shoe. I thought someone might have fallen or passed out, so I decided I'd go down and look just to be sure." She bit her lip. "He had a gash on his forehead...and his neck.... There was a bulge here." She touched the side of her neck, then shook her head. "I knew he was dead. They think he either fell or was pushed off one of the balconies."

"Jesus!" A lull fell between them for a moment. "The two detectives who came to interview me this afternoon seemed to be on top of things."

"I didn't tell them what you said, only what I'd seen. Did you tell them about his philandering?"

"Yeah. And about the woman we saw him with."

She took a sip of wine. "I feel awful for Elizabeth and her son. Because she's well-known, it will come out and might affect the charity. And the more they uncover, the more it will sully their memory of him and reflect on her, even though she's not responsible for his unfaithfulness."

He voiced the idea that had occurred to him right after the detectives left him in the conference room. "Every woman he's ever been with will be a suspect. Especially the woman he was with last night."

"I didn't notice the woman in red at dinner, but I did notice Travis's son arguing with him before the awards were presented. But teenagers are sometimes combative, confrontational. He stormed out of the ballroom. I didn't notice him returning."

"You're not saying you think his son killed him."

"No." She held up a hand, palm out, and shook her head. "But some teenagers are prone to being impulsive and act rashly when their tempers are up. And it takes some time for them to cool down. It has something to do with a rush of hormone to their brains. But the dinner went on for a couple of hours, so by the time they'd have seen each other again, his son would've had time to calm down.

"By the time the police arrived at the hotel, and after I was certain I wasn't going to throw up, I noticed something. There was a concave area on the ground below the balcony. It looked like Travis landed headfirst, and then someone dragged the body up against the side of the hotel and propped him against the wall. With his neck...I don't think he could have dragged himself there. He had to have died instantly. But he had a contusion here." She brushed her fingertips over his head above one temple. "And he'd bled onto his shirt."

"If he died instantly he wouldn't have bled," he said.

"So maybe he was struck before he was pushed off the balcony. And head wounds bleed profusely. Thanks to four brothers, I know that from experience."

"It's difficult for me to believe we slept through a fight or his fall."

She looked up. "What woke you at four?"

He'd wanted her again, but didn't have a condom. To get his mind off of the gnawing need, he'd gotten out of bed and left to go see Book. "I didn't hear a fight or anyone falling, if that's what you mean."

"Maybe the blow to his head knocked him out and they heaved him over the railing," she suggested.

"Or he could have fallen and hit his head on the railing going over. It could have been an accident."

"Or he could have hit his head and he was unsteady and fell over the balcony. But how did he end up leaning against the building?"

Every scenario brought them back to the fact that Travis was propped up against the building. The action was both caring and incriminating. Whoever was there hadn't dialed 911 or sought help, instead leaving him to be discovered later. Even if they hadn't killed him, they'd probably been worried they might be charged with something.

Sam took a sip of his wine. "The police won't be saying anything until their investigation is over."

"We'll probably hear about it on the news." She shook her head. "And it will probably be a circus. Mrs. Travis will have to plan her husband's funeral while dealing with all that."

They'd circled back into the same spot they'd been in before starting the conversation.

"I know you admire her, Moira, but what makes you think she wasn't the one who kicked his ass over the railing?"

"I could understand it if she did. But if he'd been…wandering…for some time, why would she suddenly decide to kick his ass off the balcony this time?"

"Maybe this time was different. Maybe this time meant more to him than just a quick…lay." He caught himself before using the cruder word. He leaned forward and rested his elbows on his knees. He'd wanted to beat the shit out of his father. Sometimes he still wanted to.

She rose and extended her hand. "Let's go for a walk. I've been cooped up in here since I got home and I could use some exercise. And did I tell you I got a fifty-dollar gift certificate toward another stay at the Del? I guess if you find a dead body, they don't want you to hold it against them." She shielded her eyes with a hand. "God, that sounded awful."

She was still more upset than she was letting on. Sam gave her hand a squeeze. "They call that gallows humor, and we use it to gear up for our missions. Why not poke fun at what's messing with you? It helps you shake it off."

"Thanks for understanding." They were almost to the apartment door when she said, "Elizabeth Travis asked me to do some paintings for Sarah's Dreams this summer."

He didn't like that idea. "What kind of paintings?" He'd rather she be far away from that particular circus.

"I'm not sure yet. I'll let you know when I find out."

THEY STROLLED DOWN the street to a park and paused outside the fence to watch a pick-up game of basketball. Moira recognized a couple of teenagers from her apartment complex, but didn't know the others.

Sam's features took on a hawkish, steely-eyed look as they progressed through the neighborhood. He scanned their sur-roundings constantly.

"This is a pretty safe neighborhood, Sam. I'm familiar with most of the small businesses, and we haven't had any trouble here." She looped her arm through his and leaned against him.

Some of the tension in his shoulders relaxed. "It's automatic."

What must he have experienced to automatically be so watch-ful, even in this small neighborhood?

She stroked his forearm in an effort to soothe him.

They followed the sidewalk back to the parking lot and en-tered the building. Sam stood close beside her as she unlocked her apartment door. He paused in the entryway.

"What is it?" Moira asked.

"I'm trying not to reach for you the second we walk through the door."

An instant flush of heat arrowed downward and settled in her sex. She wanted to climb him and lock her legs around him. "Sam." She cradled his face in her hands and dragged his mouth to hers.

He clamped her close, covered her mouth with his, and his tongue moved hungrily against hers.

He scooped her up. "Bedroom?"

"At the end of the hall."

He settled her in the middle of the bed and followed her down.

"I don't have any condoms, Sam. I haven't been anywhere to…"

"I brought some, just in case." He pulled a strand of six sealed condoms out his pocket.

"You're very prepared—and very optimistic."

"Just very hopeful. Now I've had a taste of you, Moira, I want more."

When he settled between her thighs, the carefully balanced

weight of his body atop hers was a welcome burden. Yet a twinge of unease struck her.

She was jumping right back into bed with him, when she couldn't be sure what he thought about her. Was that how it was supposed to be? After the experience in college, she'd never trusted anyone enough to allow them close. Until him. Had she chosen wrong?

He kissed her softly, tenderly and her heart pounded and the tension in her body dissolved. If he could kiss her like this, he had to feel something for her. Didn't he?

He lifted her long, flowing top up and over her head. With slow, lingering caresses, he explored her breasts, then bent his head to tug her distended nipple into his mouth. He drew on it, triggering a clenching heat that tumbled deep into a frantic need to have him inside her. Her hands shook as she yanked at his shirt and dragged it off, temporarily breaking the suction of his mouth.

To lie with him skin-to-skin, felt so, so right. She turned her mouth against his throat, his shoulder, and felt the tremor of response run through him. He rocked against her, the ridge of his erection in just the right spot. She moved beneath him in rising to meet the downward thrust of his body in an imitation of lovemaking that drove her pleasure higher.

Sam rolled her leggings down, following their path with kisses and nuzzles. She smelled like soap and flowers and woman. Her legs were as slim and muscular as her torso, as though she had sculpted herself. He nipped her hip, then tasted the flesh there and she shivered.

He tempted her with his fingers, finding her wet and ready for him. The scent of her arousal tested his patience, and he rose up to pull the leggings free and run his gaze upward from her feet with their pale-pink-painted toes to that flame-red patch of hair at the juncture of her thighs, then traced up to the generous swell of her breasts with their pale peach nipples, and onto her face. Her blue-green eyes looked dark and sleepy with desire.

He shucked his pants and came back to her. He guided her hand to his erection. "You don't have to be shy about touching me, Moira."

As she ran her fingertips up and down the length of him, his breathing went ragged, and he had to struggle to maintain his control. When she curved her fingers around him and squeezed gently, he couldn't hold back a soft groan. He nipped her earlobe and sucked it into his mouth. Her fingers tightened around him.

"I can't think straight while you're doing that," she complained.

"I want your hands on me, Moira," he murmured against her throat.

"Oh, God."

When she cupped his balls and rolled them gently, he covered his moan by claiming her mouth. His tongue darted forward, tangling with hers with avid need.

"Sam," she whispered when his mouth left hers. He reached for the condom and tore it open with his teeth and placed it in her hand.

"I've never done this. You're so hard and hot." She rolled the condom up over his erection.

Jesus. She was killing him. "You're warm and wet for me," he whispered against her ear as he pushed inside her.

He hesitated a moment to shore up his control, but she was already moving beneath him, driving him deeper. His movements became faster sharper, her echoing responses hurtling him over the edge. Her nails dug into his back, but he barely felt it as he spilled himself inside her.

As he lay atop her, he wondered how long something this hot could burn, because he'd never wanted a woman this much in his life.

CHAPTER 7

B OOK DIDN'T LOOK any better today than he had the past three days. His eyes were swollen from the drugs they were giving him to keep him comatose, which was a blessing. The bruising was still so bad Sam cringed every time he saw it.

Now he sat in a chair next to the SEAL's bed and tried not to look at the tubes running into the kid's nose, or the tube snaking out from under the sheet to the bag that hung from the side of the bed. The wires attached to Book's chest were less invasive, and the steady beep-beep-beep some comfort.

Even as Sam watched the monitor, Book's heart skipped a beat, then began to speed up. He uttered a low, breathy, half-sigh, half-moan that had Sam jerking to his feet. A nurse came into the room before he could push the button. "He just groaned."

"He's trying to fight free of the drugs, Lieutenant. And trust me he doesn't want to do that yet." She changed out the nearly empty bag of saline for a full one and plunged a syringe of medication into the port on the IV bag, tilting the bag back and forth, then hung it on the stand. "You're only seeing part of the bruising. It's better if he waits until some of it has faded. And after the spinal surgery they just did, he really shouldn't move."

"Surgery? How bad is it?"

A look of panic rushed across her features and she paled. "Please forget what I said. You're here so often, I thought of you as family."

"I'm as close as family. I'm his commanding officer, his team leader. He's my responsibility. How bad is it?"

"I can't say, I could lose my job, Lieutenant."

"Not if I don't report you." Aware his words fell in a shadow area between threat and promise, he took a step closer to her. "He's going to need his team. We can be a support system for him."

Her internal struggle flashed across her face. "The doctor is waiting to see if the swelling around the cord will recede before he makes a determination on whether or not he's lost all feeling from the waist down. We won't know for at least a week, maybe longer."

Fuck! Even if Book recovered feeling, the chances of him returning to his team would be slim. He might never walk again. The thought punched Sam like a fist. "Thanks for telling me. I keep secrets for a living. Yours is safe with me."

She searched his face, then seemed to accept his reassurance. "Thanks." She hurried out.

He moved to the bed. "You'll get through this, Book. We'll have your back." The only reply was the steady beep-beep-beep of the heart monitor.

Twenty minutes later Sam drove out of the parking structure and turned toward Moira's apartment. He needed a distraction, and sailing and being with her would definitely provide it for him.

His cell phone rang and he pushed the button on his steering wheel to answer the phone.

"This is your mother, Sam. Calling to make sure you're still alive and well."

He chuckled. "I'm kicking, Mom. They've assigned my team a class of SEAL candidates. We're trying to grind them down."

"But you're off in the evenings, aren't you?"

"Yes."

"I want you to come to dinner tomorrow night and spend some time with your bothers."

"I already have plans, Mom."

"You're going out on the boat today but what do you have going on tomorrow?"

"I have a date." Or he would have if he could invite Moira out somewhere.

"You have a date?"

She didn't have to sound so surprised. "Yeah. I do have them on occasion."

"Bring her to dinner tomorrow night."

Whoa! Taking a date to meet your mother was one of those things you did when things were getting beyond serious. Right now he was just having a good time—no, make that a great time—getting to know Moira and getting laid after damn near nine months of celibacy.

"Mom, we've only been out twice. And the first time was eating dinner at the same table at the fundraiser. I don't really think Sunday dinner with Tim and Trevor constitutes a relaxing meal for someone I've only just met."

"Do I know her family?"

That casual tone was how she launched her inquiry into the appropriateness of the woman. He never dated anyone he'd be ashamed to introduce to his mother, but he still hadn't introduced them. With his work schedule, the trainings, the deployments, the longest any of his relationships had lasted was six months.

"I doubt it, Mom. Her mom is a history professor at Berkley and her dad's a pharmacist. Moira teaches high school art."

"She sounds interesting. Why don't you bring her to dinner? I'd love to meet her."

"She might not feel comfortable being thrown into the lion's den on her third date. And she might get the wrong idea." Or was it the fourth?

"What idea is that, Samuel?" Her bland tone had him shaking his head.

"You know what I mean. I'm not interested in marriage, Mom."

"Have you told her that?"

"No. We're just dating."

"What's the point of dating if it isn't to find the person you want to share your life with and create a family?"

"Not every relationship has to be a quest for something permanent. There's companionship and just having someone to do things with."

A long silence followed. "You need someone in your life, Samuel. Someone who cares about you."

"I'm only here six months out of the year. I can't ask someone to wait for me every time I get deployed. It isn't fair to them."

"You're worth waiting for, Sam."

"You're a little biased." She'd made sacrifices for him and his brothers he'd never forget. Though she'd tried to hide it, he'd been very aware of her disappointment and pain when she was tossed aside for a younger model. Afterwards she ended up having to take Thomas to court and force him to pay the court-ordered child support...more than once. It still stuck in his craw that she had to embarrass his father into doing the right thing by him and his brothers. "I'll always have you waiting for me, Mom."

"You deserve more, Samuel. Don't rule out that this woman might be willing to wait for you.

And if he let Moira get too close, then deployed, then he'd probably return home to find she'd gotten lonely and jumped into someone else's bed... Just the idea had heat rushing into his face. As great as the sex was, and as attractive as he found her, he wasn't going to risk getting too close. Besides, he'd seen too many team marriages tank. And putting kids through a divorce like he and his brothers had to endure... No way.

"Is it fair to this woman you're dating that you're only seeing her to provide you with a source of entertainment?"

Her cool tone pricked his conscience. Dammit! Moira was the one to invite him back to her room that first night. She'd been just as hot for him as he'd been for her. They were two consenting adults.

But he had given her the full court press.

She'd been shaky with nerves. And so hungry for his touch. And the shy way she touched him. He could tell she hadn't had much experience, which had blown his need sky-high.

"Mom, we're just enjoying each other's company."

"Then you won't mind sharing her company with the rest of us at the dinner table tomorrow night. You haven't been here for dinner in months. And this is the first time both your brothers have been able to come. Trevor is bringing Paige, his girlfriend, and she could use some company." His mom knew exactly how to work him.

Fuck! "I'll ask Moira, but she might not feel comfortable coming. I'll call you later." He ended the call and cut loose with a string of foul expletives. He hated being guilted into family things.

WIND WHIPPED ONE of the sails until it flapped like laundry on a clothesline. Sam adjusted the boat's trajectory and the wind filled the canvas again, pulling it taut. Moira raised the camera and took a shot of the mast jutting upward and clean white fabric against the cerulean sky, with Sam standing in the foreground at the wheel.

When he originally said the word "sailboat," she imagined a small vessel with just enough room for the two of them. This was much, much, more, and she was amazed by it. The boat was actually forty-two feet long with two berths, a galley, and a very modern bathroom. The cabin below was all wood, polished to a gleaming finish, and with everything shipshape and in its place.

While Sam motored them through the harbor and out to sea, she took pictures of the water, other boats, and the harbor up close and in the distance. One particularly unimpressed egret stuck with them on the journey. Perched on the bow, he studied Moira with a bored expression while she took several shots of him from different angles, capturing him and the rich wood of the deck beneath him. Finally aggravated by all the fuss, he took to the sky, while she caught the spread of his wings against that clear, cloudless blue.

She was slowly adapting to the movement of the water beneath the boat, and as long as she avoided looking toward the horizon, her stomach didn't pitch. She'd managed to tame her curls into a ponytail and stuck it through the back of a big-billed baseball cap, although errant strands still managed to escape to dance around her face with every breeze. She was glad she'd brought a sweater, because the water-damp breeze brushed against her like clammy fingers.

She approached Sam and took several quick shots of him standing, feet braced apart, behind the wheel in the stern. "When did you buy Gypsy?" she asked as she lowered the camera.

He turned the wheel a small degree to port. "I didn't. My grandfather, my mother's father, died five years ago and left her to me."

"Oh. I'm sorry. But he obviously chose the right person to take care of her. She's gorgeous."

"I started to sail with him when I was ten. We went out nearly every weekend. Tim and Trevor were more into baseball and soccer. I loved the water. Swimming, fishing, sailing. So he left me Gypsy and left them the value in money."

So, his family had to be well off. Shit. "Is that why you went into the Navy?"

"I went into the Navy because I wanted to be a SEAL. From the first time I read about them, I wanted to be one."

"Why?"

"Because I like a challenge. I like the physicality of it. And I get to keep my country safe. And I occasionally get to blow shit up."

She couldn't compete with that. "I went into teaching to make a living so I could continue to paint. I understand the need to live your dream."

He nodded. "You're good enough to do it full time, Moira. Have you approached any of the galleries here or up the coast about selling your paintings?"

"No." Someone like him, with all the confidence in the world, wouldn't understand the stress of putting herself out there. She was still a work in progress. She'd overcome the weight problem, and learned to eat healthier, so probably it was time to tackle her confidence issues.

"Why haven't you approached the local galleries?"

"Most of the paintings I do these days are contracted pieces. They're very personal to the client I'm doing them for, so I can't create prints from them. It would be an invasion of privacy." She was making excuses. She had paintings tucked away in her cabinet she could easily peddle.

"Do paintings that are inspired by what you've already painted. You could be an artist in residence somewhere and paint all the time."

"And live on a shoestring budget that would barely pay me while I hoped my paintings sold. Believe me I've thought of it all. The day job feeds me and keeps a roof over my head. And I paint at night when I get home. Or on the weekends."

"Take the wheel for a minute." He tugged her over.

"What?" A gust of fear left her frozen. He took the camera from her and folded her stiff fingers around the wheel.

"Just hold the wheel and keep her steady. I need to make a sail adjustment." He turned the camera on her and took her picture. "And don't look so terrified. It'll be fine. Just don't make any big turns on the wheel and we'll be great." He tucked the camera in the corner of one of the padded benches that circled the boat's stern.

How was it possible to have chill bumps and sweaty palms at the same time? She was too busy holding the wheel in a death grip and keeping an eye on the waters ahead to watch while he adjusted the mainsail. Finally he sauntered back to her with a grin. "Thanks."

She whooshed out a breath when he took over the wheel and looped an arm around her waist, holding her close against his side. "I need to ask a favor of you."

"What is it?"

"My mother called this morning. She wants me to come to dinner tomorrow evening, and she wants me to bring you."

Moira studied his expression. She hadn't expected him to introduce her to his family so soon. She mulled over the way he'd asked her to go.

She should never have slept with him that first night. Because she had, it now confused the order of things. They hadn't had time to develop a stronger emotional connection. She'd be just a random woman he was bringing to dinner. And he hadn't said he *wanted* her to come.

The absence of those few words sent a clear enough message that caused her a quick pinch of pain. "Would you like some water? I think I'll go down and get some."

"No. I'm good."

She slipped away from him, scooped up her camera, and took it with her to put away. Once downstairs, she found a bottle of water she didn't really want and sat down at the table.

She had promised herself she'd never regret sleeping with him, but she did now. They had a physical connection, but she didn't know what Sam wanted...besides sex. But she knew she needed more than that. And if he didn't... It hurt. Like an empty hole had opened up inside her. She ran a hand over her face.

What had she expected? She knew when she invited him into her room that she was out of her depth. He was only four years older than her, but was more hardened, not only from what he'd seen in battle, but from his experiences as a kid and his relationship with his father.

Or was she making excuses for him? She shouldn't be. He was a grown man, a Navy SEAL. But she was torn between her empathy and her own need for his respect. Because she had sex with him that first night, the night they met, had she forever lost that respect?

She'd known all along that she was inviting him to think of her as some*thing*, not some*one*. But then there was the way he behaved that first night...so patient and careful.

Pictures along one wall of the galley snagged her attention, and she got up to scan them. They were of a man with a husky build, his hair thinning, but something in his smile reminded her of Sam. There were pictures of Sam, too. Thinner, less muscular, his smile always a little cautious, like he expected the feelings of pleasure or happiness were going to be snatched away from him.

Did he hide his emotions because he felt them so deeply? The way he kissed her last night while they made love...

She decided to believe that interpretation, because the alternative was too painful.

Taking the bottle of water with her, she climbed the steps to the deck.

SAM HOMED IN on Moira as soon as she cleared the cabin stairs. Damn it. Why the hell was she upset? It was a damn invitation to dinner. What kind of problem could that cause? Obviously a big one, because she didn't look happy.

She came to stand next to him. "I can't go to dinner with you, Sam."

Well, at least she might tell him what was bothering her. "Can I ask why not?"

"You don't really want me to go to dinner at your mother's house. You invited me because you want to please her. Not because you think enough of me to want me to know your family."

It was so close to what his mother said, an uncomfortable twinge of guilt hit him. Shit. "I was concerned you'd feel uncomfortable because you'd be dropped in a social situation with a bunch of strangers. And one of them would be my mother, for Christ's sake. And she'll pump you for info about us. She and my brothers are nosy as hell. And with both of them being lawyers, they'll interrogate you like you're a terrorist and they work for Homeland Security"

Moira laughed. "Haven't you ever taken any of the women you've dated home with you before?"

What kind of asshole would he sound like if he said no? "I haven't really had a relationship that's lasted long enough for me to be in this situation."

Her eyes looked very green behind glasses. "Why not?"

"I'm gone almost six months out of the year, Moira. And I never know when I'll be deployed. I can't really ask someone to wait for me. It isn't fair to them."

She looked away, presenting her profile to him. Against the backdrop of the water, her skin looked creamy soft. "It isn't fair to you either, Sam. None of us human beings are truly meant to be alone."

Shit, she sounded so much like his mother… "Well, do you want to brave it? Or have I scared you off?"

Her blue-green gaze shifted away again, and the glare of light on her glasses obscured the expression in their depths. He suddenly wanted her to come with him. "My brother's girlfriend will be there. I think he's going to pop the question sometime soon."

"This is a family gathering, and I'll be a random guest."

"You'll be my guest. And you might keep my brothers from starting some shit."

"Because you didn't follow in your father's footsteps?"

"Something like that."

"I'm sure you can handle yourself with them, like you handled yourself with Nelson…what was his name?"

"Clayborn. Nelson and Denise."

"She was very nice. He was a dick."

He laughed. Her prim, proper schoolteacher tone gave a special connotation to the insult. And the way she shoved her glasses back up her nose only underlined the observation.

"He and I were in law school together. He was a"—he toned down his description for her benefit—"dick back then, too."

"Why was he trying to goad you?"

"I think it was because I passed the bar on the first try. It pissed him off that it came easier for me than it did for him, and then I didn't even go into practice."

If he'd decided to follow the expected path and practice law, he probably wouldn't catch so much shit from his brothers, father, and people like Nelson. "Are you coming to dinner with me tomorrow night?"

"Yeah, I'll come. I might even have my hair under control by then. The humidity out here has made it crazy."

"I like your hair. When I run my fingers through it, it curls around them and holds on." He wound the end of her ponytail around his finger, and it curled into a corkscrew.

"That wasn't how my roommates in college described it."

"How did they describe it?"

"It doesn't matter. Are you getting hungry?"

"Yeah. A little." The way she avoided answering and quickly changed the subject made him curious. Was it something embarrassing or painful?

"I'll go down and get the basket. What would you like to drink?"

"Water. I don't drink on Gypsy unless I'm in port."

"That's probably a good idea." She disappeared belowdecks to retrieve the picnic basket.

Why had a woman so normally cautious, a woman as straight as a ruler, taken such a personal risk when she invited him to stay that first night? It seemed miles outside her comfort zone. He was finding it more and more intriguing.

And why was she so careful about the personal things she shared with him? They were sleeping together. Sure, they were physically intimate, but she didn't share anything but what was on the surface.

And he was just as guilty. His mother was right. They were spending all their time dancing around a personal relationship when it didn't get much more personal than having sex like horny rabbits and sleeping together. Or did it?

Damn it!

He wanted to know her secrets. Like what the hell her college roommates called her hair.

She brought up the basket and set it down in the open space behind the wheel. Sam set the auto pilot and moved to help her spread a blanket on the deck for their picnic.

"Don't you have to do something about that?" She nodded

toward the wheel.

"I've set the autopilot."

"Autopilot?"

"Yeah."

She narrowed her eyes at him. He grinned. "You did okay. There was never any danger with you playing first mate until I got back. I trusted you."

"A little instruction would have been helpful," she said.

Her prim tone triggered another grin. "I'll keep that in mind for next time." And there would definitely be a next time. He was going to figure Ms. Moira McKee out. "I'll show you around the boat a little more after we eat. I have some navigational maps I think you'll find interesting."

"Are they your collection of etchings?"

He laughed again. "Close enough, but I promise not to try and use them to seduce you. I'll wait for that until we're on dry land.

THE CLOSER INTO the dock Sam sailed, the less the chill breeze cut across the deck. When they were close to the marina, he lowered the sails and started the engine.

His hands gripped the wheel with easy pressure. Moira enjoyed watching him maneuver the boat, and had taken pictures of him a number of times. When her phone rang, she set the camera aside and dug into the front pocket of her backpack.

"Don't be surprised if the signal drops. It won't be stable until we get into dock," Sam said as he eased the boat over, giving a smaller craft a wide berth.

She ran her thumb over the screen and Elizabeth Travis's name came up. Why would Elizabeth be calling her? Was it to ask her about finding her husband's body? God, she hoped not.

She pressed the phone icon on the screen and put the phone to her ear. "Hello."

"Hello, Moira, this is Elizabeth Travis."

"How are you?" God, she shouldn't have asked that.

After only a second, Elizabeth said, "As well as can be expected. I'd like to meet with you tomorrow afternoon, if it's convenient."

"Certainly. I usually leave school around four."

"Why don't I come by there and meet you in your room about then?" She sounded intent, busy, in a rush.

"That will be fine. Do you need directions?"

"No, my secretary has the address and I have GPS."

"Okay. If you call me when you arrive, I'll meet you at the door and walk you back to my room."

"That sounds perfect, I'll do that. Thank you. See you tomorrow."

Moira hung up and slid the phone back into her backpack. Something about Elizabeth's tone had sounded off. But then her husband just died. And what was so important that she wanted to talk to her right away?

"Problem?" Sam asked.

"I don't know. That was Elizabeth Travis. She's going to meet me after school tomorrow."

His brows rose.

"She had talked to me about helping with a school-wide celebration for the work everyone did. But I'm not sure that's what she wants to talk about."

He adjusted. "Strange she's focused on that when her husband's going to be buried in a few days."

"Maybe she wants to stay busy so she can forget things for a while."

"Maybe. Or it might be a relief not to have to keep the pretense going any longer."

She shook her head. She still couldn't believe anyone would stay with a man who couldn't be faithful. Why put herself through that constant heartbreak?

Maybe if she got to know Elizabeth Travis she might understand.

CHAPTER 8

S AM MONITORED EVERYTHING going on on the grinder and
noted it in a book.

Being with the SEAL candidates during their first phase of
training had brought back memories of his own BUD/S experiences. In PT formation, the men strained to do the hundred or so
pushups while his men yelled encouragement and insults.

"You do push-ups like a girl, Westmore. Get wet!" Squirrel
yelled at one. The man leapt up and ran to one of the IBSs
(inflatable boat, small) and slid belly-down into the icy water filling
the boat and out the other side. He ran back to his position and
began the brutal, planned number of leg-lifts the rest of the group
transitioned to.

Twenty minutes later they were on the beach hefting the logs
again while the instructors shoveled sand at them—the point
being for the candidates to ignore the most uncomfortable
conditions, stay focused, and function as a team.

One team dropped their log and ended up taking a twenty-
minute turn in the surf. Chief Turner monitored their time in the
water, and brought them out to do flutter kicks on the beach to
warm them back up before sending them back to their log.

The morning proceeded with the usual barking, growling, and
yelling on the part of the instructors until the candidates ran to the
mess hall for lunch.

Sam walked down the beach with Frank Denotti, his team medic, and Josh Aaron, aka Arrow, one of their snipers, who was there to double-check that the candidates set up the IBSs as they should. Everything was fine, and they walked back to the class-rooms to share a pizza and sprawl out to relax. Hounding the candidates wasn't as exhausting as the harsh PT and training the candidates were going through, but they still had to stay on top of things to avoid injuries.

"Swan said you had some news about Book, LT," Arrow said.

Sam leaned forward in his chair and rested his elbows on his knees. Book and Arrow were swim buddies during training, and they also hung out outside of training and deployments. Even knowing that, Sam still felt he needed to be up-front. What he had planned wasn't going to be easy for them.

"He's going to need our support." He understood what he was asking of his guys. It was hard to commit to offering con-sistent support to an injured comrade, because by the grace of God it could be one of them. Every time the men saw their teammate unable to fall back into his position, they were reminded of the dangers of what they did and the toll it could take on their bodies and lives, personal and professional.

"When Elijah landed, he broke his femur and he bled for a long time. They haven't brought him out of the medically-induced coma because he broke his back as well, and he's bruised all to hell from his chest down. When they bring him out of the coma, they may find that he's got brain damage. And even if he's okay cognitively, he may be paralyzed from the waist down, and may never walk again."

"Jesus," Denotti breathed…half expletive, half prayer. He ran his fingers through his dark hair, long on top and nearly shaved on the sides.

Arrow tossed his empty bottle into a trashcan with more force than necessary. The bottle bounced out and hit the wall. He ignored it and moved to one of the metal framed windows to look out, every muscle in his back and arms stiffened. "I've been there every day, and no one told me about his back."

Sam understood the emotions bombarding the man, and decided to give him something else to focus on. "Have either of you seen or talked to Alisha?"

Arrow turned from the window and his expression bore the stress of emotion held in check. "I have. She's at the hospital most mornings. She's waiting tables at one of the restaurants in the Gaslamp Quarter and trying to keep it together."

"What about his family?"

"His mom's staying at his apartment with Alisha. They're visiting him in shifts and staying as long as the hospital staff will let them."

Sam's mother being on staff in the cardiac unit gave him more flexibility, since he was a familiar face there. His late and early visits were probably why he hadn't run into either of the women.

But how long would Alisha and Book's mother be able to stick it out? People had to live, had to make a living, pay their bills.

His men would feel better if there was something they could do for Book.

"Arrow, can you act as a go-between for us with Book's mom and Alisha? Find out if they need anything, and if there's anything the team can do to help out?"

"Sure."

"Good. Let us know as soon as you can."

"Roger that, LT."

"Let's hit the beach."

The three of them walked out to the grinder and over the burn to the beach. Sam rested a hand on Josh's shoulder, holding him back. Though he'd asked Swan straight-up, he'd decided to ask Arrow about his attitude. "Do you have any clue what the hell was going on between Book and Swan?"

"Swan didn't think Alisha was good enough for Book. But Book had other ideas."

"What about you, Arrow?"

"It was really none of my business, LT. But if Book was happy, I was good. We're friends and teammates, but his home life is his business. He and Alisha were both eager to get hitched, and she was looking for a better-paying job so she could help more with the living expenses. Book said she was crazy excited when she landed this waitress position because the tips are good. They were both looking toward their future together. And she seems crazy about him."

If Swan was right about her background, Book might be the first guy who treated her like a person instead of a piece of tail.

"Let me know what we can do as a team. If they need money, we can pass a hat."

"Roger that, LT."

MOIRA INVITED ELIZABETH to take a seat at one of the art tables and took the stool across from her.

"I appreciate you taking time to see me today," Elizabeth said.

The woman seemed to have aged ten years since Moira last saw her. Her hair was simply swept back from her face into a ponytail at the base of her neck, and her perfectly applied makeup couldn't hide the lines of strain around her eyes and mouth.

"You're welcome. I was going to fix a cup of tea. Would you like one?"

"That would be lovely. Thank you."

Moira went to the cabinet behind her desk and got out two coffee mugs, filled them with water, put a teabag in each, and popped them into the microwave. She got out the small carton of milk from her dorm fridge, a bottle of honey, and a few packets of sweetener, some napkins and spoons, and put everything into a supply basket.

"I don't keep any cookies or snacks here." She returned to the table with the basket.

"That's okay, Moira."

The microwave dinged and she retrieved the mugs and brought them to the table and took her seat.

She tore open a sweetener packet and added it to her tea then stirred.

Elizabeth added honey to hers. "What do you do during the summer?"

"I usually paint all summer. I have four commissions lined up for the first three or four weeks."

"And you have mine as well." Elizabeth smiled.

"Yes, I haven't forgotten."

"Do you have a portfolio of your work I can look through?"

"Sure. I usually keep a scanned image of the pieces I do for other people and the ones that come through inspiration." Moira slid off the stool, went to her desk, and retrieved the album. "I can show you an original I just finished for someone. It's for a couple's sixth anniversary. The husband will be here to pick it up tomorrow."

"I'd love to see it."

Moira went to the closet where she kept her student's canvases and got out her painting, positioning it on the easel next to her desk.

For a long moment Elizabeth gazed at the work, her expression closed. When she turned her head to look at Moira, tears glazed her eyes. "It's amazing. Beautiful and sensual and amazing."

"Thank you."

"You have the spark. There are a lot of people out there who can draw and paint, but few who have that creative genius that sets their work above others. I believe you have it." Elizabeth patted her arm.

Touched, Moira glanced away to keep from tearing up.

"What kind of painting should I choose for Sarah's Dreams?"

"I have some ideas. Why don't you let me work them up in pastel, and then you can choose which one you like the best?"

"That sounds perfect." Elizabeth took a sip of her tea. "I know you have a full plate this summer with your art, but I was wondering if you'd have time to work part-time for me. My assistant will be leaving in five weeks, about the time you'll be finishing off the last few days of school. I need someone to take her place until I can find a full-time replacement. I was wondering if you'd be available to fill in for two or three weeks."

Stunned, Moira remained silent for a full minute or more. "Why me?"

"I talked to your principal a long time the other night. He said you were the driving force behind the fundraisers and the organization that went into it. I think you'll be able to drop right into the position without a hitch. And I'm hoping I might sweet-talk you into settling into it full time. And if not, then we'll have a chance to get to know each other and you'll have time to do the painting I'm commissioning."

"I'm flattered you want me to work for you, but..."

Elizabeth placed a hand on her arm and leaned forward in her chair. "Don't dismiss the idea out of hand, Moira. I know you're settled in here. I know you're a gifted teacher and painter. That painting," she tilted her head toward the easel, "is stunning. But you could bring a creative outlook to Sarah's Dreams that's been missing. What you did with the fundraisers was masterful."

"It took an army of teachers and students to do it. The whole student body was involved. Next year they're going to try and do something similar to raise awareness for art and music education and for more technology and funding in schools in those subjects. It's a real-world education for them to see what goes into economic projects. And they see where the money is spent after it's raised. They're even going to be part of the process of choosing what is purchased with the funds."

Elizabeth leaned back and smiled. "I can already tell I'm fighting a losing battle. You won't want to miss all that. But what would be your dream job if you could choose it?"

That was easy. "To paint full time. It's what I've always wanted to do. To make a living from my art. I wouldn't mind doing workshops and even teaching classes a couple of days a week. But to paint full time would be a dream come true."

"Come to work for me a few weeks this summer, and we'll use the painting you do for us to raise awareness of the benefits of art education in schools. Maybe that will jump-start your dream. And raise money for the art department at your school and others."

The idea that she might be able to get statewide exposure was too good to be true. And usually when something sounded too good, there was a catch. "Why would you do that for me if I can't promise to work for you?"

"Because I created Sarah's Dreams to promote the dreams of children and students. You try to promote that every day here at school. We'll just take your dream and give it a wider scope. But I want you to share your expertise with my team, and that's the whole point of you coming to work for me, whether it's for two weeks, or longer. I don't think you really appreciate what you achieved here, Moira. I really don't know how you managed it."

She took a sip of her tea. "And my team is working on the celebration for your student body. I didn't want to delay it since you only have five weeks before school lets out. I thought a concert. What would the students think of having Loud and Unbound here to play? They've just released their second album, and it's taking off. They used to play at one of the bars in the Gaslamp Quarter, but now they're touring, and they're looking for some performances at charitable events to give them some exposure. Your school would be perfect for that."

"I think the student body would be wild about it. What did Mr. Jacobs say?"

"He was excited about it, but he wanted you to have the final say."

"Really?"

"Yeah. He knows how much work you put into the program here."

"The student body would be over the moon with Loud and Unbound. But I think the football field definitely. There will be more space for the general public to attend."

Elizabeth smiled "Mr. Jacobs thought so too. He also suggested that you could advertise it locally and sell tickets to the general public and kick off your next year's art and music programs with a little cash."

"What a terrific idea. Will the band be okay with that?"

"They're looking for a cause to help raise money, so yes, I

think they will."

Moira reached for a sheet of paper. "We'll need to rent chairs or mobile bleachers to utilize the field, because the stands aren't nearly big enough. And we'll have to have porta-potties because the facilities won't handle larger crowds. And we'll have to hire private security. Some food and drink vendors."

Elizabeth chuckled. "He said you were great about looking at the big picture and breaking it down into what was needed to get the job done."

She took one last sip of her tea and rose. "My offices will be closed for the next week, but you can call me on my private line when you make your decision about the position." She reached into her purse, took out a business card and wrote a number on it.

Moira abandoned her list. Her mention of the office being closed brought them back to her husband's death. Something Moira felt they'd both been skirting since Elizabeth's arrival.

"I'm so sorry about what happened to your husband, Elizabeth."

Sadness flickered across Elizabeth's face, and her eyes sheened with tears for a moment, but she pulled it together. "My son Michael and I will get through this. We have each other to hold on to."

"If there's anything I can do, just ask."

Elizabeth shook her head. "The police are investigating. We have to give them time. I was so exhausted after the dinner, I went straight to bed and didn't know he hadn't come back to the room until the police knocked on the door the next morning." Elizabeth shook her head. "I can't imagine anyone wanting to purposely hurt him. It has to have been an accident."

"I hope they have answers for you soon. I know this has made it more difficult for you, during a time you need to process it all and grieve. I appreciate you trying to take care of this for the kids, but you need to take care of you and your family first."

Elizabeth rested a hand on her arm. "This has given me something else to focus on, and a respite from sitting at the house and wandering from room to room. I'm better if I have something to do."

Moira certainly understood that.

"When you found him…"

Moira swallowed. She was bound to ask. "He'd been gone a while. I don't think he suffered. I think it was a very sudden thing."

"Did something wake you?"

Moira's cheeks felt hot. "A friend spent the night with me in my room. When he left for work, he woke me and I got up. It was nearly daybreak, so I wandered out on the balcony. That's when I noticed something white close to the building, and nearby what I thought was a shoe. I went in, got dressed, and went out to see if it was someone who needed help."

Elizabeth gripped the handle of her purse with both hands. "I know it must have been a shock."

"Yes, it was."

"Thank you for telling me."

Moira nodded.

"So, are you and Sam dating?"

Moira cheeks heated at the question. "Yes."

Elizabeth chuckled. "You shouldn't feel embarrassed. He seemed very focused on you that night. He's smart, and he obviously knows quality when he sees it. I hope it works out for you both."

She started to defend what they'd done that night and suddenly decided she wasn't ashamed of reaching for what she wanted, what made her happy. "We're getting to know each other." And she was finally coming out of years of painfully low self-esteem and shyness.

"I'll walk you to the entrance," Moira offered.

"You don't need to. I can tell you have some things to finish up on. I can find my way."

As she watched Elizabeth Travis walk away, Moira wondered if she'd been pumped for information, been played, or if she should feel flattered that Elizabeth wanted to hire her. She couldn't really put her finger on what set off her wariness. Perhaps because Elizabeth somehow seemed overeager to have her at her headquarters. Why would she want to work with someone who'd found her dead husband? Since Moira discovered his body, wouldn't she be a constant reminder of his death?

She needed to give all of it some thought before seriously considering the job.

And she had other things to worry about. Like meeting Sam's family tonight at dinner.

CHAPTER 9

S HE SHOULDN'T BE nervous. She wasn't Sam's girlfriend. They were dating, but they hadn't cemented their relationship in any way, and they hadn't even agreed to being monogamous. Which she already was, and she believed he had been so far.

This whole relationship thing was so confusing.

All her worries and confusion raced around in a mental hamster wheel as they neared Sam's mother's house. She wiped her sweating palms on her slacks.

"There's nothing to be nervous about, Moira."

Sam wore a tan dress shirt with blue and gray pinstripes. The color somehow brought out the tawny lights in his eyes.

Her heart sped up as she studied his features.

"What is it?"

"Nothing. No, actually, I'm wondering if you'll be so relaxed when you meet my family."

She laughed at the quick jerk of his head in her direction and felt a little steadier.

They turned into a neighborhood of impressive homes and eventually into the driveway of a sandstone-toned brick, two-story mansion that sprawled across the lawn like a sleeping lion.

Moira hoped the imagery didn't follow her inside. "Beautiful house."

"Mom got it in the divorce settlement, since she paid for most of it, and she had us. She's remodeled a little since we left home. Lately she's talking about selling it because it's too big for her alone, and maybe buying a condo so she doesn't have to take care of the yard."

Large yucca plants surrounded by stones and smaller bloom-ing flowers were arranged in a landscaped area between the house and the front steps. "Does she do her own landscaping? It's beautiful."

"Some of it. I've done some of the work now and then when she needed a strong back. When Trevor and Tim were both in school and I was deployed, she hired a guy. He's been doing it the last couple of years."

Sam opened the front door for her and stood back to allow her to precede him. A tall woman entered the hall from a room on the right. Dressed in a sleeveless navy blouse and a white skirt that flowed around long, muscular legs, she was built like a runner—strong, fit, and slender. She had Sam's unusual caramel-toned eyes, but her hair, cut chin level, was lighter and streaked with blonde.

"Sam, I'm so glad you're here, and you must be Moira." She offered her hand, and Moira shook it automatically. "You must call me Chelsea. I'm so thrilled you could join us. Come in and have a drink before dinner and meet the rest of the family."

Sam placed a hand against Moira's waist, guiding her into the large open room that was a combination of both living and dining room, with part of the kitchen visible beyond the dining area.

A couple sat on the couch. The man, she assumed, was Tre-vor. His resemblance to Sam was pronounced, but his eyes were a dark, flat brown. When he rose to shake Moira's hand while his mother introduced her, she noticed other subtle differences. He was a couple of inches shy of Sam's six feet, and his shoulders were narrower. "This is Paige, my girlfriend," he said.

Paige was blonde, blue-eyed. and gorgeous, and her smile was genuine. "Lovely to meet you. We've never met any of Sam's girlfriends."

"So he's told me."

"Probably because he has to resort to escort services or personal ads to find one." Trevor said with a smirk.

Chelsea gasped and Sam's hand tightened at Moira's waist.

"Trevor…" Paige's distressed expression and tone must have gotten through to him.

Moira glanced up at Sam. An intent, predatory anger lit his tawny eyes. Was that how he looked when he went into battle? The controlled violence in his stance promised instant action.

"You need to apologize to Moira, Trevor." Sam's quiet tone sent a shudder through her. The tension hung thick between the brothers, and she found it hard to breathe.

Trevor turned to look at her, and his brown eyes looked through her as though she wasn't there. "I apologize, Moira."

She couldn't accept the apology. Being called a whore by a stranger had been a shock. His total lack of sincerity made his rudeness something far worse. She had no idea there was such animosity between Sam and his brother.

"Moira and Sam met at the Sarah's Dreams dinner at the Del," Chelsea said, filling the silence. He attended as a favor to you and your firm, to deliver your donation."

"Not your usual kind of gig, was it, Sam?" Trevor's smile didn't reach his eyes, nor did he offer Sam any thanks.

"I made it through without embarrassing the family."

Trevor's mouth tightened. Sam's double-edged retort must have hit the mark.

"We sat with Nelson and Denise Clayborn, Estelle and Joe Patterson, and Doris and Landon Thompson. The Pattersons and Thompsons are still clients, aren't they? I don't think Clayborn tried to poach them. But you might want to check."

Moira bit her lip at his obvious needling.

A man wandered in from the kitchen with two wine glasses. "Hey, Sam." He put a two-thirds filled white wine goblet on a coaster on the table at Chelsea's elbow.

"Tim, this is Moira. Moira, my baby brother. He's the newest lawyer in the family."

"It's nice to meet you." He smiled. "I'm acting as bartender tonight. Which would you rather have, white wine or red?"

Her throat felt dry. "Some ice water would be good."

"Coming right up. Your regular, Sam?"

"Nothing, thanks."

While Tim went into the kitchen to get the drinks, Sam guided her toward the second couch in the room and they took a seat. Moira tried to relax but couldn't completely control the instinctive need to draw into herself.

Chelsea, Sam's mother, settled in one of the chairs facing the fireplace and took a deep breath. "Sam said you teach."

"Yes. High school art."

"How long have you been doing that?" Tim asked, as he placed a glass of ice water in a coaster on the table in front of her. He sat in a chair parallel to his mother's.

"Six years."

"You must have the patience of Job," Paige said.

"Sometimes. And at other times it's a joy."

"What sort of artwork do you do when you're not teaching?" Trevor asked.

She almost flinched at his voice. "Portraits, landscapes, children. Mostly they're personal requests by the clients that commission them."

"So, you're building your name. Is that why you were invited to the fundraiser?"

Moira had wanted to accept this invitation with an open heart, and to like the people in Sam's family, but she didn't think she'd ever like Trevor. He was a predator looking for someone weaker to prey on. Had he learned that before he started law school, or after going to work for his father? And why on earth was Paige with him? "No, my school raised a sizeable donation, and my principal asked me to collect the award they gave us."

Sam's mother leaned forward in her seat. "How much money did you raise?"

"Twenty-five thousand."

"That's—amazing," Paige exclaimed. "How did you do it?"

She didn't really want to go into it again, but couldn't really refuse. She explained about the fundraisers, the students, how they had turned it into a school-wide mission.

"And your family?" Tim asked.

She caught Sam's pained expression. He had warned her. She briefly outlined what her parents and siblings did.

"So, two of your brothers are artists, too," Chelsea commented.

"Kyle, the youngest, is coming along as well. I gave him a camera last year for his birthday, and he seems enthusiastic about it, but then most teenagers take pictures all the time."

"Paige does, too. I think every moment of our time together has been documented," Trevor commented.

There was an indulgent tone in his voice and attitude that struck Moira as condescending.

Paige made it plain it had affected her the same way when she said, "My photographs have saved you embarrassment more than once, Trevor. No one's memory is perfect."

Moira bit her lip again.

"I was only teasing, babe."

Paige continued as though she hadn't heard him. "I want to be able to look back and say, I remember that. And since I can't paint, I'll have a photograph for Moira to work from if I ever want a portrait done."

"Do you ever paint yourself?" Tim asked.

He didn't seem to have yet acquired Trevor's arrogant attitude. Maybe he wouldn't.

"No." She shrugged. "I'm not an interesting subject."

"That's not true," Sam said. He'd been silent beside her. When he spoke, everyone turned in his direction.

"A man of few words," Tim said dryly. "As always."

Sam raised a brow. "Too bad I can't say the same about the rest of the family." He focused on Trevor, and his brother smirked.

Trevor turned his attention to Moira again, and her stomach tumbled. She'd seen that kind of fake friendliness on her college roommates' faces, right before they proceeded to torment her again. "Where did you go to college?"

The innocent question only heightened her wariness. "UCLA."

He was like a dog with a new bone he wanted to gnaw clean as he questioned every aspect of her education and dissected her answers.

When he started in on her career choice, it was frighteningly similar to what she'd experienced in college, the conversation spoken in a friendly, conversational tone, but with that undercurrent of bullying.

Moira's hands and face felt numb. She knew she was hyperventilating, but couldn't control it.

"If you're such a gifted artist, why aren't you out there selling your paintings."

"I do sell my paintings."

"Obviously not for enough. Otherwise you wouldn't be teaching school."

Sam was suddenly on his feet. "God dammit, Trevor. Enough. We're leaving, Moira."

Relief threaded through the anxiety, and Moira rose, her legs stiff. The need to escape the room overwhelmed everything else.

Chelsea, Sam's mother, rose as well. She looked as exhausted as Moira felt. "Sam…"

"You can't take responsibility for him for the rest of his life, Mom. He's a grown man."

"Hey…" Trevor half rose, but sat back down when Paige grabbed his sleeve.

"Moira." Chelsea's throat worked.

Moira swallowed and tried to pull herself together. "It was nice meeting you, Mrs. Harding."

Sam grabbed her hand and tugged her around the coffee table. He turned before they got to the entrance foyer. "Paige, if you marry my brother, you'll be making the biggest mistake of your life. He wasn't teasing about the photos. And you're too smart to put up with his shit."

"God damn you, Sam," Trevor jumped to his feet. "Don't listen to him, Paige."

"You don't deserve her, Trevor. You've turned into *him*, and she doesn't need someone like you in her life, any more than Mom did. No woman does."

Trevor lunged from the couch with fists bunched as he stalked toward Sam. Sam stepped forward to meet him. Trevor swung a fist. Sam dodged back, and the blow barely grazed his chin. Sam's quick jab connected solidly with Trevor's nose.

Trevor yelped and blood splattered across his shirt. He covered his face, bent at the waist, and groaned several times. "God damn you, you son of a bitch. You've broken my nose. I'll have you fucking arrested for assault."

"No, you won't, Trevor," Chelsea shoved him back onto the leather couch while Tim rushed in from the kitchen with a towel that Chelsea used to stanch the flow of blood. "You struck him first, and I'll tell the police exactly that. You've done enough damage for one day. Tilt your head back."

"Let's go." Sam tugged Moira toward the front door.

Paige rushed into the entrance hall. "Can I catch a ride home with you two?"

"Paige. You can't leave." Trevor's tone sounded nasally since Chelsea still held the towel to his nose.

"Yes, I can, Trevor. I've given you so many chances to be a stand-up guy, but this was the final one. I don't know why you feel you have to spread around your father's anger for him, but that's what this was about.

"You weren't having a polite conversation. You were interrogating Moira like a criminal. You were trying to tear her down in front of Sam, and you started the moment she walked into the room. And it made me sick to watch it."

Her breathing hitched and her eyes shimmered with tears. "You treat me the same way, Trevor. You have to tear people down so you'll feel like the big man. All it shows me is how small you really are. Don't call me again. And don't come around my apartment. I'm done."

Paige jerked the handle of her purse over her shoulder and led the way out of the house. Once the door closed behind them,

Moira drew a shaky breath, and Paige turned and embraced her. "I'm so sorry," she murmured, her voice trembling.

"Me, too." They clung together like accident victims.

Once they were in the car it took a few minutes for Moira to force herself out of the protective stupor she'd slipped into. Her movements jerky, and she tucked her hands between her knees to still their trembling. She'd felt...stifled by Trevor, like every bit of oxygen was being sucked out of the room and a lead weight had been dropped on her chest. Just as she had in college when her roommates did the same kind of thing.

Because she was different back then, an art student, and fat, they decided their rudeness and insensitivity were acceptable. She'd been an easy target, and they picked on her, and did cruel things, unforgivable things, until she cleaned out her room and left. With those memories riding her afresh, she crossed her arms and pressed her trembling hands beneath them while looking out the window and concentrating on blocking out the memories and releasing the tension that made her neck and shoulders ache.

The drive to Paige's apartment was accomplished in silence. When Sam pulled the car to a stop, Paige reached over the seat and rested a hand on Moira's shoulder. "I'm sorry, Moira. You showed more grace under fire than I could ever have done. I hope you won't hold Trevor's behavior against me. If you ever want to get together, give me a call, and we'll go out for coffee." She dangled her business card over the seat.

Moira grabbed it. The woman was not only friendly, but unbelievably brave to have broken things off the way she did. "I'll do that."

ONCE MORE ON the road, Sam passed up the exit leading to her apartment.

"Where are we going?" she asked.

"To the beach. I thought we'd take a walk."

Moira nodded.

"I'm sorry, Moira. I should never have taken you there."

She wished he hadn't. It stirred up memories and pain she'd worked years to put behind her.

Sam parked at one of the restaurants and came around to open her door, then gripped her hand as they made their way down to the beach.

HOW COULD HE ever make this up to her? How could he ever erase what his brother did? "I teased you about my brothers treating you like prosecutors. It never occurred to me Trevor would really go after you, Moira. He hates my guts, but I've never seen him so intent on—"

He stopped. Her pale, calm composure worried him. Was she in shock? Probably. "I wanted to beat the shit out of him for you, Moira."

"You'd have ended up in jail. That one punch was humiliating enough. And he lost Paige."

His anger eased down a degree and he squared his shoulders. "Don't let what happened today come between us."

She looked away and remained silent a moment. "I know you're not your brother, Sam. You've built your whole life around protecting people."

He rarely felt helpless, but right now, with this cardboard calm she'd wrapped around herself, he was stumbling around in the dark. She was going to end things now if he didn't do something. But what?

He wrapped her in a tender hug. He felt resistance in every muscle in her body for five seconds, then ten, until she slowly melted against him and her arms went around him, and he could heave a sigh of relief.

When she nestled closer, the knot of tension in his belly started to unravel, until he realized she was crying. Shit! He hated when women cried. He didn't know what to do. Helpless as hell wasn't one of the conditions he aspired to. For lack of a better idea, he continued to hug her.

She moved out of his arms and brushed at the tears trickling down her cheeks. Her eyes looked as deeply green as the ocean when she tilted her head back to look up at him, then away again. "I think I need to lie down for a little while."

"Okay." They turned around to walk back to the car.

He wanted to break through the distance wedged between them. Rip it aside. But doing anything at this moment might cause more damage. If he took her home right now, though, she'd end things, and he'd never see her again. He sensed it, felt it in the sickening pitch of his stomach.

He didn't want them to end. Thus far they'd barely dipped below the surface. He wanted to know what made her hold back from him, everywhere but in bed. She said she'd only slept with one other man. Had she been this way with him? Sharing her body, but keeping everything else tightly bound. Or was she tightly bound because of him? The question added a new level of pain to the mixture of anger and regret churning inside him.

Once in the car, he turned the vehicle toward his apartment near base. He needed time for the trauma she'd experienced to numb. He needed time to figure out a way to reach her again before he took her home.

The building was older, but the rent was reasonable, and he had an extra bedroom where he stored all his gear. He hadn't done much by way of decorating other than buy a few pieces of furniture. She was surrounded by color, art, and beauty at her place. What would she think of his utilitarian lifestyle?

"Where are we?" Moira asked, interrupting his thoughts.

"My apartment." He opened the car door and went around to open hers before she could ask him to take her home.

She accepted his hand and allowed him to help her out of the car. "I don't spend much time here." Was he trying to warn her, or making an excuse for his lack of interest in the place? He rarely brought women here. He usually ended up at their place. He wasn't going to delve into his reasons for that.

They rode the elevator to the second floor, and he guided

Moira down the hall to his apartment. The living room seemed barren in comparison to hers, though he had a large couch and matching chair arranged so people could see the television he rarely watched. An end table sat diagonally between the two pieces of furniture and a coffee table was centered in the middle of the large green and burgundy rug, something his mother bought for him. The pillows at each end of the couch matched, another of her gifts. He'd left the floor lamp lit for when he returned, but the light did little to brighten the space. He crossed through the kitchen to open the drapes that covered a sliding glass door leading out onto a small balcony. Light spread across the floor and dispelled the gloom slightly.

"Can I get you something to drink, Moira?"

"Some ice water."

She wandered into the kitchen with him and went to the sliding glass door to look out. "How long have you lived here?"

"Four years."

"You don't have any pictures on the walls."

"I haven't been here very much. I've been deployed a lot."

She pushed her glasses up her nose in a gesture he'd learned signaled stress.

He handed her the water glass. "Maybe you could help me choose something that would fit."

She took a sip. "Are you asking because you really want to hang something because you're interested in having something pleasant to look at, or because it looks as though you just moved in."

There was the wry humor he loved so much. "Both."

"You could bring some of the things you don't use on the Gypsy and hang them. They'd be something familiar and comforting."

Comforting? He hadn't thought that he needed comfort. Why would she think he did?

"One of the navigational maps you showed me on the Gypsy would be nice. You could frame one that means something to you, and arrange it with something nautical."

"That's a good idea." And it would be simple to get it framed.

"Some pictures of your grandfather would be good as well."

"You noticed those?"

"Yes. Your smile is like his."

"My mother says that, too."

"I'm glad you had him, Sam."

"I am too." Was she waiting for him to explain what happened at the house and why?

"It's difficult for me talk about things, Moira." He ran a hand back and forth over her shoulder and down her back. "My father left when I was thirteen to go live with his girlfriend before the divorce. I snuck out one night and slashed his tires, and they caught me on camera on the street outside his girlfriend's apartment. He had me arrested and put in a holding cell overnight as punishment, then dropped the charges the next morning.

"I understood the need for punishment. I destroyed private property, but I decided then that he'd never have control over my life ever again. When he came to pick me up the next morning, I refused to go with him. I baited him, calling the woman he was sleeping with names, and calling him some, too. He lost his temper and hit me in the face with his fist, knocked me down in clear view of several police officers. He was arrested for child abuse, and we ended up in family court. I didn't see him again until I graduated from high school."

"Is that when you started to cultivate that Hard Ass Harding reputation?"

His face felt stiff as he smiled. "I guess so." He caught her hand in his. "I imploded what little relationship I had with my father, Moira. And because of what I did, Trevor and Tim didn't get to see him much either. It's affected us all in different ways. Trevor was eleven, and every time Dad didn't show up for a visit with him and Tim, he blamed me. And since he's been working for Dad his animosity toward me has gotten worse."

"What about Tim?"

"Tim was only nine. Things didn't seem to affect him as much. And so far he's not buying into Dad's mind games."

"I wonder what makes people do that, instead of stating straight up what they want."

"They're cowards and are afraid to come out with it. In my father's case, he's intent on punishing me for not buying into his shit." He shook his head. "With Trevor, my father doesn't expend any effort to exert his control. Trevor pretty much does whatever Dad tells him to, and he thinks tearing people down gives him the power Dad denies him."

She remained silent for a moment. "You could be right." She turned and went into the living room and sat down on the couch. He followed her there, wondering if she was ever going to forgive him. She found a cork coaster and placed her water glass on it.

"It isn't easy for me to share private things either." She looked up. "We have that in common."

She sucked in a deep breath. "In college, my sophomore year, I had three roommates. I didn't choose them. It was one of those things where you move into an apartment with other people to share the expenses. I was very shy then. I suppose I still struggle with that. I didn't have many friends in high school, and none who were attending UCLA.

"The three other girls were friends from the same school." She swallowed. "I moved in, and at first things were fine. I was busy with my classes and wasn't at the apartment much because I was busy at the studio. And they were friendly enough. Then things started to change." She swallowed and looked away.

"They started to make comments about me, how I dressed, how I looked, how I talked, walked, everything I did." What she ate. She fell silent a moment. "And they'd say it in just the tone Trevor used when he was discussing my degree. It escalated to the point that I avoided being there as much as possible."

A hollow sickness settled in Sam's stomach.

"Everything came to a head when one of them damaged a sculpture I'd worked on for weeks. It was to be part of a show there at the college. And part of my final in the class.

"She apologized, but she wasn't sorry. I figured she'd done it on purpose, and I told her so. She didn't even try to defend herself. I was able to repair it, but the situation was too much for me.

"I moved out that night, while they were out at a club, and slept in my car for nearly a week until I found a notice on a board at the student center. Someone looking for a roommate to share expenses. Her name was Sandra Cane, and she was as much an outcast as I was, and had gone through nearly the same experience I did.

"It took us nearly a month before we stopped avoiding each other, which isn't easy to do in an apartment the size of a postage stamp. But we're still friends even now.

"I found out a month after I moved out that my ex-roommates had invited another girl from their high school to room with them. And that's when I knew everything they put me through was so they could force me out and make room for her."

Jesus! "Guys would have just gone out behind the building and fought it out. Winner take all."

"Yeah. I could always depend on it being a straight up fight with my brothers when they had a disagreement. It's usually women who can be more devious and spiteful."

"Have you seen any of them since then?"

"I did while I was in school. But I never spoke to them again. Since we graduated, I've tried to put it all behind me. I have better things to do with my life than to relive any of those experiences." She drew a deep breath.

But she'd just been through something very similar, while sitting in his mother's living room. And it had forced her to live through it just now. Damn Trevor! The urge to get in the car, drive back to his mother's house and break his brother's fucking jaw to go along with his nose stormed through him.

She surprised him when she said, "Poor Tim. I have a feeling he was doing most of the cooking, and we walked out before he could feed us." Maybe we could invite him and your mother to my apartment for a meal."

Something inside him unclenched, and he cupped Moira's face and kissed her. "Thank you for offering. It's very generous considering what just happened. But I think even I need some space from my family for a few weeks."

She bit her lip. "I don't want Trevor around me ever again, Sam."

He couldn't blame her. "I'm good with that." There wouldn't be any reason for the two to meet again.

"Whatever your father and brother have done, they're your family, Sam. You may cut them both out of your life eventually. But you'll always have regrets unless you at least try to resolve things between you."

"Life's too short to keep toxic people who make you miserable in your life, Moira. I hadn't seen Trevor in almost six months."

"It broke your mother's heart for him to behave as he did."

"Only he can do something about that, if he even cares."

He couldn't understand Trevor's behavior. It wasn't like they were in competition for their father's attention especially he didn't give a shit if he ever saw the man.

And as for money… Sam knew he'd never see a dime from his father, and that his estate would go to Tim and Trevor. What little would be left after the side piece got her share. He was okay with that.

But this animosity his father had sparked between them needed to stop. She was right about one thing. He, his father and Trevor needed to resolve some things, and once he'd faced things head-on, he'd visit his father's office and settle things once and for all.

CHAPTER 10

MOIRA OPENED HER eyes to the beep-beep-beep of a backup alarm on some kind of machinery, possibly a garbage truck. Morning light shone through the blinds and she angled her watch to see what time it was. Four-thirty. She rolled out of bed and went into the bathroom to take care of business and get a drink, and eased back into bed for a few more minutes.

Emotionally and physically exhausted, she fell asleep some time after dinner while watching a movie with Sam. She woke up in the middle of the night and found him sound asleep beneath the covers beside her, while she was fully dressed and covered by a separate blanket. Undressing down to her panties and camisole, she climbed in with Sam went back to sleep.

The shock and the hurt of Trevor's attack was still there, but it had dulled somewhat. It could be one of those invisible scars she carried with her if she allowed it, or she could lay it down and dismiss it. She'd learned a long time ago that clinging to the hurt feelings and outrage triggered by other people's treatment only hurt her, not them. She needed to set it down and walk away.

But Trevor would always be Sam's brother, and if she and Sam continued to see each other she refused to become a dividing force between them. They needed to resolve things between them. They were family.

Sam's warm male body cuddled close against her from behind,

the hard length of his erection pressing against one cheek of her ass. Intimate areas of her body responded like he'd flipped a switch. His hand moved beneath her camisole to stroke and caress, intensifying the ache of need centered between her legs. When his lips caressed her shoulder, she bit back a groan.

"You okay?" he whispered against her ear, his deep voice a rumble that sent delightful shivers through her while he used his fingertips to toy with one distended nipple.

"I'm okay." She wiggled around to face him. Even with his short hair sticking up in spikes atop his head, he was sexy as hell. She smoothed his hair and kissed him softly. "I could be better." She ran the backs of her fingers over his belly to the waistband of his boxer briefs and beneath.

The light of desire in his eyes flared and his pupils expanded, making the tawny tones of the irises to darken to burnt sienna. She curled her fingers around his erection and caressed him the way she'd learned he liked.

"You keep that up and I won't be any use to you," he said huskily. He kissed her. His hand surfed over her skin until he tucked it in the back of her panties and traced the rounded curve of one cheek of her ass, then the other, while he nestled her in close. She latched onto his earlobe, gave it a tug, and felt his shudder.

She wiggled free of her panties and he wasted no time shucking his boxer briefs. When she rose and straddled him, he gripped her waist.

"Condom," he reminded her. She leaned over to pluck one out of the box on the nightstand. She turned all her focused on his bold, smooth, very erect cock while she slipped the condom over it. "Out of the numerous penises I've seen…I think yours might be exceptional."

One dark brow rose. "I was under the impression you hadn't seen that many."

"Well, after studying six thousand years of art, I've seen drawings, sculptures, paintings, photographs… and I've drawn nudes from live models." She bit back a giggle. "I'll have to tell you about that." She lowered herself over him, welcoming him inside her, and goosebumps trailed over her skin at the sweep of pleasure being connected to him always gave her. "I think you might stand the test of time."

He laughed, then tugged her down and kissed her with a deep, slow intensity that stole her breath and left her throbbing with need.

"We'll see how long either of us lasts," he murmured as he raised his hips, deepening their connection.

She was addicted to this. Addicted to his special way of guiding her toward orgasm like he instinctively knew just how to touch her, how to move. She lost herself in making love with him. His hands trailed over her bare skin as though he wanted to touch every inch of her, even while his hips rose to counter her downward thrust.

They caught a slow rhythm, stretching out the pleasure until it was agonizing to remain poised on the brink. She tumbled over the edge, and as the throb of Sam's release pulsed inside her, a feeling of tenderness and contentment flooded her. She rubbed her cheek against his.

"I like the rest of you just as much as I do your penis."

He chuckled. "I can't get enough of you either." He brushed back her hair and drew her down for another kiss, his lips tender. There was something in his face that made her heart beat hard and fast.

THE CHALLENGE OF getting to work on time was settled when they shared a shower, and Sam dressed while Moira struggled to tame her hair.

She was still fiddling with it when he was ready, so he turned on the television to pass the time while he waited. Finding a news channel, he tossed down the remote. Denise Clayborn's face flashed on the screen, and he fumbled to get the control to turn the volume up. "Mrs. Clayborn was found shot to death in her car last evening at her home." A picture of Denise holding a little girl popped up on the screen.

Moira hurried into the room to stand beside him, her eyes on the image.

"According to a police spokesman, the investigation is ongoing, and no suspects have been arrested. Her family has asked for privacy to process and mourn their loss. She is survived by her husband of six years and their three-year-old daughter."

"God, that's horrible," she whispered softly. "I only spoke with her for a few minutes, but I thought she was nice."

"Yeah. she was." He'd seen death in combat, but always distanced himself from it. He couldn't afford not to. But this was someone he knew, had laughed with, broken bread with. She was young, had a child...

"Wonder what happened?"

Sam shook his head. "They live in a gated community. It could have been robbery, but I can't imagine anyone gaining access to the place to do it."

Moira reached out to touch Sam's arm. "I'm sorry, Sam. I know you knew her before the dinner, had a history."

"Since college. That's where she and Nelson met."

"I feel bad for her family."

"I do too." They'd both been talking about what a dick Nelson was just the other night, and now he'd lost the one person who made him a little less of a dick. Denise had been a positive influence on him. It seemed strange that a tragedy had struck another person they'd both seen just days before.

"Should we do something?" she asked in the elevator as he punched the button to take them to the lobby.

"Like what?"

"Send a card or take by a meal or something."

"I'll have my mom check with Nelson and ask."

Because she seemed so concerned, he tried to distract her while they walked to the car. "What have you got planned for today?"

"I'll be working late, getting ready for my end of the year art exhibit. I need to get some of the display boards and tables out and hang some of the artwork."

"I can come by and help out a little after five."

"Thank you! I'd love the help."

MINDFUL OF THE time, Moira was anxious to get out of the car and slung her purse over her shoulder. Sam caught her sleeve and leaned across the console to kiss her. "I'll see you around five thirty."

"Okay."

Moira rushed inside to change clothes. Ten minutes later she walked back out wearing slacks and a bright pink top. She approached her car, then slowed as she caught a glimpse of it. Her heart sank. The dark blue exterior of her used Civic was covered with white splatters. She moved closer. It was paint, and still wet. She turned one way, then another and scanned the area around her.

Who would do this?

She reached for her cell phone and started to dial Sam. Then stopped. He didn't have time to deal with this. She didn't either. She dialed her school and let her principal know she'd need someone to cover for her until she had the car towed.

Next she dialed the police.

SAM LOOKED FROM one man to the next as they filed into the classroom used for SEAL candidate instruction and briefings. His team had been on the beach running surf passage all morning, and now the BUD/S class had slogged off to the mess to eat, they had time for Lt. Commander Yazzie's sitrep.

Swan, Bullet, and Denotti sprawled in chairs. Gilly hiked a hip on the edge of one of the desks, while Arrow and Squirrel stood at the back of the room.

"Lieutenant Commander Yazzie will be here shortly," Sam said. "I went by the hospital this morning, and they're easing Book out of his coma now. He was groggy and talking like he was drunk, and he looks like hell, but the docs don't think he has any brain damage. They haven't told him about the paralysis, and I don't think he's aware enough to realize it on his own."

"God!" Rosenburg murmured from his position at the door. His ran his fingers through his dark hair, pulling it back from his face. "It might be a blessing if they just keep him doped up for a while longer."

Sam aimed for a calm, positive tone. "It might not be as bad as we're thinking, Squirrel. He's a SEAL. He won't give up, he'll work to come back from this." He scanned the faces of his team. "We all owe him the best support we can give him."

Gilly Giles chimed in, "Hooyah, LT." Gilly, with his surfer dude shaggy blond hair and scruffy cheeks, was unwavering in his determination to complete the mission, whatever it was. He'd do whatever it took to get the job done. Sam could depend on his enthusiasm to inspire the rest of the team.

"Attention!" Rosenburg snapped, and the entire team leapt to their feet.

"At ease," Lieutenant Commander Yazzie said as he strode up the aisle between the desks and moved to stand at the front of the room. Yazzie was a large man with the bearing of someone who carried the weight of command comfortably, and he had the reputation for being a solid, no-bullshit operator.

"Take a seat." He tossed his folders on the desk planted center stage at the front of the room and within easy reach of the markerboard.

The men standing at the door at the back of the room made their way forward and slid into seats.

Yazzie lifted a chair and flipped it around to face the men, then sat down. "The assessment on Book's parachute has come back." He leaned forward to rest his elbows on his knees. "The findings are that there was nothing wrong with Book's parachute. The lines tangled, keeping it from opening. The investigators couldn't tell for certain if it was caused by the chute being packed incorrectly, or if it got twisted after it was deployed. Book released his main chute and deployed his reserve. It opened but, as you all know, it was too late. He was only four hundred feet from the ground when it released.

"Every parachute on base has been checked. Two chutes were found to have defective ripcords. So, though the outcome for Book isn't any better, his accident has possibly saved two other team members from experiencing a similar issue."

He shifted in his seat and straightened. "I've been in touch with Book's family. His medical team thinks he's going to make it. And they don't believe he has any brain damage from the landing or the blood loss. But there will be long-term effects from this accident. He has some feeling in his toes, but that may be all he recovers."

A sinking sensation hit Sam's stomach. He knew what was coming. Had wondered when it would happen.

"As shitty as all of us feel about this, and for him, I have to transfer someone in to take his place. You need to be a cohesive team the next time you deploy, and that means you need eight able-bodied men. I'm going to give you three files, Sam. You can interview each operator and see who you think would fit in with the team. I've vetted them myself, and they're all solid men."

His pale gaze swung toward the rest of the men. "Whoever ends up with the team, he'll be here to do the job, the same as the rest of you."

In other words, don't give him any shit for not being Book, or for taking his place.

His guys always behaved professionally, but this was going to be an emotional transition. Book was the youngest in their group, and the other men had taken him under their wings like a kid brother. They'd all developed a close relationship with him.

How many guys had he worked with who'd transitioned out because of injuries or died in combat? Quite a few. But never one in a training accident.

Yazzie rose, and every man stood. Yazzie handed Sam the

three files. "You have a week to make a decision."

"Yes, sir."

Silence followed the Lieutenant Commander's exit.

Squirrel went to the window and looked out, the light emphasizing his slightly hooked nose and dark brows. "I knew it the moment I saw him going down."

Sam shook his head and tried to offset his own emotions. "He's going to live, that's the important thing."

Swan shifted and stuck his hands in his short's pockets. "He lived and breathed being a SEAL, LT. It's going to be hell for him."

As it would be hell for any of them. They ate, slept, drank, and breathed the life. He'd done that for the past four years.

But thanks to Moira, his world was changing. She was creative and open to ideas and adventures. And she showed an unusual empathy for people, in dozens of ways.

"He'll adapt, Swan. There will be other important challenges he'll face while rehabbing from this, and he'll do it. But he'll need plenty of support from his family, his friends, and his team." He scrubbed his hand over his hair, roughing it up. "It's hard for us to see him like this. Hard to face that it could be one of us. But how much harder would it be if we just walked away without offering a hand after he's been part of our team for so long? You don't leave a man behind, no matter how hard it is to go back for him."

For several days he'd been trying to come up with some way to help Book.

Sam turned to Swan before he could reply. "What would you do if you couldn't be a SEAL anymore?"

Swan paused mouth open, and shrugged. "I don't know."

"That's a question every one of us needs to ask ourselves. What we do now may be the only thing we've ever wanted to do. But when we separate from it, what will we do? Lie down in a ditch somewhere and give up?

"We plan our missions down to every last, tiny detail, but we live our lives in the moment, with no thought of the future. We need to start looking toward our futures while we're living our lives."

"That's easy for you to say, LT. You have a law degree," De-notti said.

"I didn't get a law degree because I wanted to practice law, Denotti."

"Then why did you?"

None of them knew about his past. "Because my father is a bastard. Every dime he gave my mother in child support she had to take him to court to get. He did it to purposely fuck with her. And I wanted to make him pay. You know how much college and a law degree costs?"

Denotti shook his head.

"Four years of college and four years of law school, two hundred thousand, and that doesn't count living expenses. It had to be a law degree in order for him to pay for it. Then I got the added satisfaction of walking away and joining the Navy."

"He's a lawyer, isn't he?" Bullet asked.

At Sam's nod, Bullet shook his head. "So, you got the law degree just to fuck with him?"

"Yeah. The day I passed the bar I enlisted."

"Shit," he breathed. "Remind me to never get on your bad side, LT."

Sam flashed him a grin. "Being a SEAL was always the plan, but there was no guarantee I'd make it. So, I got a college degree to hedge my bet. Making him pay was the icing.

"When I leave the teams, old, gray, and beat up, I'll move on to something else."

The guys laughed.

Sam sighed. They'd turned a corner before it could spin out of control. "Our mission now, where Book is concerned, is for all of us to encourage him to reach for something else while he's recovering. He has to see there can be a life outside the teams. A life where he can use the skills he learned here with us. If he has something to concentrate on, he'll heal faster."

"What do you suggest, LT?" Arrow asked.

"Let's sit down and see if we can figure something out."

CHAPTER 11

MOIRA CHECKED OFF the first item on her list, tickets for the Loud and Unbound concert. The printer had finished the first run and she just distributed the tickets being sold in the office as well as by students. Luckily that had been her only duty for this particular school project.

She was fighting an uphill battle to keep her mind on getting things done for the concert and her art show because her ruined car kept popping into her thoughts, distracting her with worries about who did it, and why. The super hadn't noticed it when he arrived at work at seven. And no one else reported seeing anyone dump paint on her vehicle last night. The paint was still wet, so it had to have happened just before she arrived home from Sam's apartment.

The cops had asked if any of her students were pissed off with her. But none of her kids would do this. She had a few struggling in her art appreciation class, but none doing badly enough to trash her car.

Thank goodness the cops helped her get her car towed to a garage where they could steam the paint off before it dried and permanently damaged the finish. She'd have to pick it up tomorrow.

In the meantime, she needed to get some of this done. Second thing on her list was dragging the display boards and tables out of

the storage room so she could set up the art show. She hustled
down the hall and loaded two of the tables onto a cart, and she'd
just gotten back to the room when her phone rang.

"Ms. McKee, there are some gentlemen here to see you,"
Emily, one of the two school secretaries, said.

"More than one?"

"Yes." Her voice dropped to a hushed whisper. "I haven't
seen this much eye candy in one place since my best friend Stella's
bachelorette party in 1992. We went to a strip joint on lady's night.
You can take your time getting here. I'll entertain them."

Moira laughed. "I'll take my time." She was still smiling as she
walked down the hall to the office, but slowed as she reached the
four girls leaning along the wall gazing through the large, tempered
glass window into the office. Moira recognized all four of them as
cheerleaders.

"I wonder what they're doing here?" one said.

"Who cares? This is the closest we're likely to get to Navy
SEALs in this lifetime unless we enlist."

"How do you know they're Navy SEALs, Cynthia?"

"I've been on the beach close to where they train. The instructors wear those shorts and t-shirts."

"Ladies, aren't you supposed to be somewhere?" Moira asked.
They all four jumped. "Practice maybe?"

The blonde, Cynthia, jerked her wrist up to look at her watch.
"Oh, shoot. Mrs. Hacker's going to be pissed." The four took off
down the hall at a trot. Moira didn't bother to call them down for
running.

When she swung the door open and entered the office, she
saw Sam sitting in the third of the office's cheap beige plastic
scooped chairs lined up against one wall. Two others slouched in
seats close to him. All three jumped to their feet as she approached them. The men were equally matched in height, broad-
shouldered, muscular, and dressed in tight blue T-shirts and shorts
that hugged their powerful thighs. All three wore sneakers, and
sunglasses hung from the neckline of their shirts.

Testosterone saturated the air. It smelled like sun-kissed skin and man.

Catching the wide-eyed look on Emily's face, Moira had to stifle a giggle.

"Hey," she said as she reached Sam. His tawny caramel-colored eyes settled on her, and she immediately felt a quick flash of pure lust that sent heat south.

When she reached him, he looped an arm around her and she fought the urge to lean into him too closely, conscious of Emily's rapt attention.

"This is Frank Denotti, and Josh Aaron, Moira."

Denotti leaned forward and extended a large hand. His dark hair was buzzed on the sides, but the top was longer and had some curl. His warm green eyes were startlingly light beneath heavy brows. "It's nice to meet you. You can call me Denotti."

Aaron, in contrast, was blond and blue-eyed, his hair a little longer and just shaggy enough to curl. He had the sculpted body of a swimmer...they all did...but Aaron was less bulky with muscle than Denotti. She bet he could glide through the water like a dolphin. "I'm Arrow," he said with a grin.

"It's good to meet you both."

"Denotti and Arrow volunteered to help set up the display boards for your art show. We can get them up in half the time."

"Really? You don't mind helping?"

"Naw. We're good," Denotti said, flashing dimples that probably had the women swarming him. She thought she heard Emily sigh behind her.

"The boards are in the storage room. They're all on wheels, but there are a lot of them."

The three men fell into step with her as she left the office and walked down the hall to the storage room in her wing.

Sam said, "We've been invited to eat at a friend's house after we get through here. Spur of the moment, if you're game."

"Sure. Is that why you brought reinforcements?"

He flashed her a smile. "Yeah."

The men rolled the panels out of the storage closet and down the hall like they were nothing, when it usually took two boys to each panel, and her making the trips with them all the way to supervise. When they reached the common area outside the wing, she stopped them. "I've put tape on the floor to mark where we need to place them. I can do that if you guys can keep bringing them out for me."

She demonstrated by unfolding one, placing it exactly on the tape markers, and locked it in place.

"This looks like a major undertaking," Sam said after his third trip.

"It is. But I'll have the students hang their work as they come in tomorrow and it'll be done in nothing flat."

Sam shot her a look.

"Yeah, okay. I know." She waved one hand. "Some of them have done it every year and they can help the ones who are new to it. I have all the mat boards to mount them on, and we'll deal with that first before we do the rest. It'll work out."

A rush of excitement hit her. She hadn't shared the news with anyone yet, having just heard it from the two students. She'd been saving it to tell Sam. Since his men were out of the room, she curled against him, and he automatically slid an arm around her waist. "I have two students who've been offered scholarships based on their artistic talent and their test scores."

His smile broke out giving her that rush it always did. "That's great, Moira." He hugged her and brushed her cheek with a kiss.

"I'll show you their work after we've got these display panels in place. And I have something else I'd like to discuss with you when we're done with this." She toyed with straightening the way his sunglasses hung from the neckline of his T-shirt and rested her hand against his chest, just because she couldn't resist. Touching him was becoming an addiction.

"Okay. We saw the signs outside for the concert."

"Yeah. The band was looking for a local charity to support, and we're going to use the money we raise to purchase technology and materials for the music and art programs here."

"Is this the thing that Elizabeth Travis set up?"

"Yes. As a thank-you to the school."

"That's great. I bet the kids are excited."

"Yeah. They are. This close to the end of school, it makes it feel even more like we're sitting atop a powder keg. They're already over it and just want these last two weeks to be done. So do the teachers."

"Including you?" he added.

"Yeah, I'm tired." She rested her head against his shoulder for a moment.

When Donatti appeared down the hall pushing another group of displays, she took a step away, and Sam went to help them while she straightened out the accordion-folded display panels and locked them down.

Sam was right. The three men worked as a team like they were connected by some kind of invisible network and had the panels set up and locked down in a quarter of the time it would have taken her.

While Sam took over placing the panels, she started hanging large pieces that had won awards in state contests on one panel. Because they were hung before, they were already set up for display.

Denotti and Arrow sidled up behind her and studied the pieces.

"Those are damn fine drawings," Frank said.

"Thanks." She straightened the pastel drawing of a man playing a violin. The gleam on the surface of the instrument, the tone of the man's skin, seemed so realistic she half-expected him to take a breath. "This one won a statewide art contest, and the student who did it has received a scholarship at UCLA."

"How long you been teaching?" Arrow asked.

"This is my sixth year."

"You must be doing something right," he said.

"Thanks. I've been fortunate to have students who have talent to work with and are motivated to cultivate it."

The two men shared a glance. "Do you have anything here that you've painted?"

"There's one in my classroom. You can walk down to see it if you like. It's down that hall." She pointed toward the hallway on the right. "Fourth door on the left. The painting is hung on the bulletin board behind my desk."

The two wandered down the hall, leaving her alone until Sam pushed the last board into place and sauntered over to her. "These don't look like students' work, Moira. They look professional."

"Dana and Thomas are very serious about their art. She works from her own photographs, but he does a lot of on-site drawing and painting." She hung one of Thomas's pastels at the other end of the board. They would get top billing with all the awards posted.

"A teacher like me is lucky to score a few really gifted students in their career. I've taught two in these last four years, and they've both earned scholarships to college."

She drew out a pastel of a guy, arms crossed, leaning back against a 1964 Mustang convertible, the reflective shine on his sunglasses mirroring the cloudless blue of the sky. She could almost feel the breeze moving his white hair. "This is Thomas's great-grandfather. He bought the car as soon as it came off the assembly line. Kept it in his garage, babied it, and left it to Thomas's grandfather. His grandfather, who's still living, gave it to his dad."

"Sweet ride." Sam moved in close against her back, looped his arms around her waist, and pressed his cheek to hers.

Moira's heart drummed against her ribs, her legs went weak as cooked spaghetti, and her mouth grew dry. She swallowed so she could speak again. "Yeah. He used photos he took himself to draw the car, but he drew his great-grandfather from memory. He died last year at age eighty-five. He plans to do a drawing of his grandfather and father leaning up against the Mustang in different poses. And then himself when it's his turn to own the vehicle."

"Quite a legacy."

"Yeah."

She started to tell him about her car but hated to ruin the moment, so decided to mention it later.

"I'd like to paint your boat." She turned to look over her

shoulder and up as she said it. "And you. If that's okay."

"Me?"

"Yeah. When you're behind the wheel or working a sail, you're part of the boat. It's like an extension of you. The painting wouldn't be complete if it didn't include you."

"Are you going to put sunglasses on me like the kid did his gramps?"

"I will if you want me to. Is there a reason you want them?"

"We try to avoid pictures that show our faces, Moira. We hunt terrorists for a living, and if they were able to identify us, it could easily make us or our family targets."

She hadn't thought of that. She was discovering things about him every time they were together. "I'll use the sunglasses."

"Hey, LT! You gotta see this," Denotti called from her classroom door.

Moira picked up the few pieces she hadn't hung yet and brought them to the classroom. She'd do them tomorrow along with everything else. But then getting ready for a show was always difficult and time-consuming.

Aaron was standing at the table with the clay work the students had done this year, hand-built and thrown, while wire sculptures were carefully displayed on a shelf, and abstract wood sculptures assembled from cut wooden shapes were clustered on a table against the back wall.

Denotti and Aaron prowled the space and seemed to be taking it all in.

"You're going to need a small army to get all this stuff transported out there in the commons area, Moira," Sam said his eyes narrowed as he scanned the room.

"I have seventy studio students who'll help with it. And besides, they need to learn how to display their work. It's part of the process."

He wandered around the room "This is impressive."

"The paintings are stored in that closet over there." She pointed to a door in the corner. "This cabinet is actually supposed to store architectural plans, but one of the parents donated it to my program a couple of years ago for us to put our drawings in."

"Do the kids sell their work?" Arrow asked.

"Not yet. I've been searching for a shop that could carry some of our clay pieces and sell them to raise more money for the art program. And we have weavings the Art 1 students do that are really remarkable this year."

"Sam said you do paintings on the side."

"Yes. I've been doing a couple of paintings a year to fund my program."

Sam's turned at hearing that. "You shouldn't have to buy materials for your classroom, Moira."

"In a perfect world, schools would be fully funded, Sam, but they're not. My students need materials if they're going to experience art the way they need to."

"You'll get some money from this concert. Maybe that will fund your program for next year."

"Maybe. If we do well."

Arrow stopped before the painting hanging behind her desk, a beach scene with sunbathers under umbrellas. The pale tan sand looked like it might burn feet if anyone walked across it barefoot, but the blue-gray shadows the umbrellas cast over the reclining figures created the cooling point of the painting. She'd taken the photo at the Del. "How much do you get for a commissioned piece?" he asked.

"It depends on the size of the canvas and the subject matter. A painting twenty-four by thirty-six about two thousand. Thirty-six by forty-eight would be between three and four thousand, depending on the subject matter."

Arrow turned to look over his shoulder at Sam. "How many personnel you think come on base, LT?"

"Possibly ten to twelve thousand. That's reserve, active, and student population."

"What if you did a painting for us, Moira, and we put it up at the main office to raffle off? If everyone bought one ticket for, say, a dollar, even if you just got half the personnel on post it would add up to six thousand."

"We'll have to check with command first and see if there're any regulations against it, Arrow," Sam said. "If there aren't, I'll talk to the Captain and see what he says."

"What sort of painting do you think would be popular with the base population?" she asked.

Sam raised a brow. "Most of the population on post are male. What do you think?"

"I'm not painting a nude, Sam."

Sam and Denotti laughed. Arrow said, "Well, shit."

"I'll come up with something."

"It would be good if she has red hair like yours." Denotti said, a teasing light in his eyes.

Moira's cheeks heated and she turned to Sam. "Do you guys have an office or some place you meet regularly?"

"Yeah."

"I'll do something for just your team as well as something more mainstream for the fundraiser."

Denotti and Arrow grinned and bumped fists.

She shook her head. Guys never changed.

"What else can we do?" Arrow asked.

"I could use some help moving the pottery to the tables. I have that cart with the edge on each level to keep them from falling off. Once they're placed, I'll have the students make labels and arrange them."

Moira's cell phone rang and she reached for it. "There's another one here waiting for you," Emily said.

"He's come for his painting. I'll bring it down to him." She crossed to her desk and retrieved the envelope holding the photos Hawk Yazzie had given her.

"I have to go take a painting to the office. I'll be right back to finish up." She went into the classroom storage closet and retrieved a box.

"I'll carry the box down to the office for you, Moira," Sam volunteered.

Moira, glanced in Arrow and Denotti's direction and bit back the words, *please be careful.*

Arrow shot her a thumbs-up. "We got this."

The Lieutenant Commander was leaning against the counter at the desk. Emily's cheeks were flushed, and she was grinning at something he was saying. When he saw Moira, he straightened to his full six-foot four height and smiled. His features, so strongly imprinted by his Native American heritage, made her fingers itch for a pencil, or perhaps charcoal. His gaze trailed past her to Sam.

"It's good to see you again, Lieutenant Commander Yazzie. Do you know Sam Harding?"

"Yes, I do." He extended his hand. "Sam."

"Sir." They shook hands.

"You'll want to see the painting before I seal it for transport," Moira said.

Emily rose from her seat behind the counter and leaned forward, obviously interested.

Sam turned the box so she could slide the canvas free, and Moira propped it on one of the chairs.

Yazzie remained silent for several long moments, his expression unreadable while he studied the painting.

Moira's stomach tightened. "If you're not pleased…"

He raised a hand, cutting her off.

"I'm very pleased, Ms. McKee. I'm stunned that you were able to take what I said, and with the help of a few pictures, turn it into this."

She smiled relieved.

"Zoe will be thrilled with it, though I had it painted as much for me as I did her."

"It's your anniversary, too."

"Yeah." He broke into a smile. "I'm a lucky man. She rarely sees herself as others see her, but I think you've captured that special quality she has that attracted me to her the moment we met."

That was high praise coming from a man who probably had very exacting expectations from all the men under his command.

"I'm so glad I was able to fulfill your vision."

Hawk extended his hand, and she took it. He held hers for a

moment, and his gray eyes focused on her, so pale in a face bronzed by the sun. "You are very gifted. Thank you."

His praise, so sincere, had tears pricking her eyes, and she blinked rapidly. "Thanks, and you're welcome."

"These are the photos you gave me to work from." She extended the manila envelope.

He smiled as he handed her a smaller envelope. "Payment in full."

"I'll email you a receipt from home."

"Sounds good."

With Sam's help she slid the painting back into the box and taped it shut.

Yazzie turned his attention to Sam. "See you on base."

"Yes, sir."

"He's your commanding officer." Moira said as they walked back to her room.

"Yeah. We had a meeting today about Book's accident. We'll have to transfer in a replacement for him next week."

"Any change with Book?" After listening to Sam talk about the man, she felt a connection to him even though she had never met him.

"They know he's going to live and he doesn't have any brain damage, but he's lost most of the feeling in his lower extremities."

Though on the surface he showed little emotion, she knew he was very concerned for the man. He'd stopped by to check on him every morning for days.

This was someone he'd fought beside in combat, someone he trusted, and with whom he'd trained. "I'm sorry, Sam."

"I am too."

She tugged him to a stop "Is there anything I can do?"

He shook his head. "No. I wish there was."

On impulse, she cupped his face and kissed him.

They drew apart at the sound of feet coming down the hall.

The four girls who'd earlier been gawping at Sam and his team guys outside the office strolled down the hall with three others. All were loaded down with gym bags. Cheerleading practice was over.

Sam drew her closer against him, his hand against Moira's waist, giving the group more room to pass.

A voice came from behind them. "Way to go, Ms. McKee!"

Laughter shone in Sam's eyes as she giggled.

Her cell phone rang and she pulled it out of her back pocket. She recognized the garage's number. "I need to ask a favor. I had some trouble with my car this morning, and I need a ride to pick it up."

"No problem. What kind of trouble?"

"I'll tell you on the way."

CHAPTER 12

"THIS IS THE floor," Sam said as he exited the elevator and snagged the door to hold it for an orderly pushing a man in a wheelchair.

He gestured to Gilly and Swan to follow him.

"Who called to tell you he was awake?" Gilly asked.

Swan answered, "Alisha. She said she thought he might need us to come by and visit. He's taking the news pretty hard."

"Who the fuck wouldn't know that?" Gilly muttered, his features tightened in an angry scowl. "This fucking blows."

Dammit. Book didn't need to hear the things running through his own head voiced by someone standing on two good legs. Sam grabbed Gilly's arm. "You do *not* say anything that isn't upbeat and encouraging as hell. Is that understood, Gilliam?"

Gilly's anger dissolved and he looked away. "Yeah. Yeah, it's understood."

Sam released him. "Stay out here until you have your head on straight."

Sam beckoned to Swan and they continued down the hall.

They both stopped outside the door. Sam glanced at Swan, and Swan gave him a thumbs-up. Sam tapped, then pushed it open.

Book lay prone on the bed, a thin pillow beneath his head. He turned look at them, and desolation in his eyes punched Sam squarely in the gut.

Alisha turned from the window, country-girl pretty with her strawberry blonde hair and cornflower blue eyes. Sam could understand why Book had fallen for her. She'd been at the hospital every day since Book's accident, but Sam could tell it was wearing on her. When she turned to greet them, she chewed on her bottom lip until it turned berry red, and her skin looked pale and her lips chapped.

"Why don't you take a break and go get something to eat, Alisha?" Book said. "You need a break and the guys will be here with me."

She went to the bed and gripped his hand. "Would you like me to bring you back something to drink? The doctor wants you to drink lots of fluids."

"Sure. That'd be good."

"Would you like juice or—"

Book cut her off, an edge to his voice. "Anything will be fine."

"Okay." She gathered her purse and rushed out of the room.

A lengthy silence followed after her exit. Sam broke it. "How are you feeling?"

"I don't feel anything."

"Doesn't mean you won't. You have to give your body time to recover from the trauma, Book. It's only been a little more than two weeks."

"It won't make any difference."

Sam leaned over him and braced a hand against the head of the bed. "I know you've had a hard knock—"

Book interrupted. "Why didn't you let me die?"

"Because you were still breathing, still fighting. You're one of my men. We looked for you for over an hour. We didn't give up on you. We don't leave men behind."

"I'm not a SEAL any longer. I'm not one of your men."

"You're wrong. I don't abandon my people. You'll be one of my men until you take your last breath, Book."

Sam caught a flicker behind the deadness in the man's eyes.

Swan crowded in on the other side of the bed. "You'll be a SEAL for the rest of your life. You may not be able to go into combat, but you'll come back to do something else. Probably more important than going on missions with us."

Gilly opened the door and strode in. Picking up on the tension in the room, he sauntered forward to stand beside Sam. "You look better than the last time I saw you, man. You're coming back."

"You guys were here while I was out?"

Gilly shrugged. "Well, outside of being on base training other guys, yeah. Where the fuck else did you think we'd be?"

"I figured you'd be too busy hunting tail, romantic devil that you are, Gilly."

Swan laughed, then snorted.

Book's smile was faint, but it was real. Sam heaved an inward sigh.

"Hand me the bed controls, will you?"

"You had that cleared by the docs?" Sam asked.

"Yeah. I can't do too much more damage sitting up. They've got enough hardware in there to hold a train together. You guys can take a seat and stay awhile, can't you?"

"We wouldn't be here otherwise," Gilly jabbed.

Sam handed Book the controls, and he raised the head of the bed to a slant.

There were only two seats, so Gilly leaned back against the clothing locker.

"I remember releasing my main chute, and pulling the rip cord on the backup, but I don't remember anything after that."

"We hunted for an hour while we waited for search and rescue, and I found your main chute about half a mile from where you came down. By then the choppers were there actively searching. You'd lost some blood from the compound break to your leg when I found you. As soon as I puffed smoke, they landed and had you loaded and out of there in a matter of minutes."

"The docs said it was close. The only good thing is I can't feel the leg or the bruising so it doesn't hurt."

"How's Alisha doing? She was pretty cut up when they brought you in."

"She's okay." Book covered his eyes with a hand as he struggled to maintain his composure.

Swan laid a hand on his shoulder. "The two of you will find your way, Book. You need to go ahead and get married. You could do it right here at the hospital. The guys and I can help you set it up."

Book jerked his hand away, his gaze raw with anger. "After you rode my ass about it before, now you're going to push for us to get married. No. I can't ask her to take this on, Swan."

"If you'd been married already, she'd be taking it on, wouldn't she? You can't just leave her high and dry, Book. She gave up her apartment. She lives with you. She loves you."

"I won't let her wipe my ass or bath me like a baby."

Sam saw where this was going. "First of all, you're not helpless. You can do your own ass-wiping and bathing. Work the problem, Book."

He gave the man a moment, hoping he'd break free of the self-pity again.

"You don't need to make any major decisions right now. You need to give it some time."

"That's all I'll have now, LT. Time."

"And you'll need every minute of it to learn how to get mobile again. You have a future, Book. You can piss it away by playing the pity card, or you can grab it by the balls and fight your way to it. That includes your life with Alisha. The only easy day…"

"…is yesterday," Book finished. "This is different. I may not be able to be a husband to her."

"You got two hands and a mouth, don't you?" Swan said.

"Hooyah!" Gilly said.

Book shook his head and even blushed at their levity.

His father's disloyalty was never far from Sam's mind. "There's more to being a husband, Book. Your dick doesn't promise love, loyalty, and respect. You do. Alisha's been here every day, standing by your side. She wants you to live as much as the rest of us do. She loves you. Don't throw that away. You're going to need it, and her."

As though on cue, Alisha eased the door open and peered around the edge.

Sam glanced at his watch and got to his feet, and Swan followed suit. Gilly straightened from his slouch against the clothes locker. "We've got to get going. We've volunteered to be security for a high school concert. It's an end of the school year thing."

"LT's girl raised a bunch of cash for a charity and as a thank-you, they arranged for Loud and Unbound to play at the school to raise money for next year's art and music programs."

Book's brows rose. "I didn't know you had a girl, LT"

His girl... His teammates were calling Moira his girl. "We're just dating."

"She's an art teacher. A damn fine artist, too," Swan said.

"You'd better watch Swan. He sounds smitten," Book warned.

"She wouldn't put up with him for a New York minute," Sam said and extended his fist. Book bumped knuckles with him. "We'll be back."

Book looked up at Alisha as she placed a bottled soft drink and a juice on the hospital table pulled across his bed. "Thanks, hon."

That "hon" gave Sam a small scrap of hope that Book wouldn't push her away just when he needed her most. "If you two need anything, call."

Her smile was uncertain. "Thanks."

Inside the elevator the three of them slouched against the back of the car in silence all the way down. "You did good, LT. I think he was in a better place when we left." Gilly said just before the door opened.

"Only for the moment, Gilly. But we can't do all the work for him. It's mostly up to him. We just need to give him a boost now and then."

★

JUST AS HE started to pull out of the parking slot, his phone rang, and he glanced at the screen. Tim rarely called, and when he did it was almost always something important. "Hey, Tim. What's up?"

"Any chance you could run by the office today? I have something I want to discuss with you."

"I can come by now."

"Great. See you in a few."

Sam's jaw worked as he turned his car toward his father's offices. He'd cooled down from his run in with Treavor, but he had zero desire to see his brother or his father. Maybe he'd get lucky and avoid them both.

Moira's car being splattered with paint seemed so similar to his taking his rage out on his father's car, he'd wondered more than once if Trevor might have been responsible. It would have taken very little effort to find out where Moira lived and what car she drove. Sam couldn't completely rule it out, any more than he could say it was anyone else, and he'd run through all the possibilities more than once. Someone at school pissed at Moira for a failing grade, a random act of vandalism done by passing teenagers, or...what other motivation could the vandal have? Why her car out of all the others in the parking lot?

He was seeing connections to them meeting both Mark Travis and Denise Clayborn where there were none. But something was triggering his radar and making him itchy. And it hadn't started until Denise was killed.

There still hadn't been an arrest, even though nearly four weeks had passed.

He left his car at a nearby parking structure and walked down two blocks to the office. The firm was housed in a building with several different professional practices—a psychologist, a dermatologist, a dentist, an engineering firm, and his father's law firm.

The lobby was all highly polished floors and a security desk, and the man working there was new and didn't know him.

Sam waited while he called upstairs to check that he could be admitted. What did it say about their relationship when he had to wait in the lobby instead of being put on some kind of list that allowed him on the floor?

What would it say about them if he was refused entry?

The idea had barely registered when the security guard hung up the phone. "You can go on up. You know the way?"

"Yes, thanks."

He held the door for two women, one pushing a baby stroller, and then climbed in himself. The baby grinned at him, drool running down his chin. He had the urge to wipe the kid's face.

He wondered if his dad had ever done that, or even changed a diaper when they were babies. Probably not. But that wasn't what they'd missed, anyway. It was the expectation of caring they had been denied. They'd been like possessions to him, and just as disposable. His sons as long as they were toeing the line, and, even worse, when they weren't, his mother caught the flack.

And that was a major part of the resentment and rage he felt toward Thomas Harding. His father had moved on with his life after marrying the side piece, and left them behind, but he'd still been critical of the way his mother raised them. Thankfully, two of the three of them had grown into regular guys, but the third had turned into as big a shit as Thomas.

The elevator door opened and his father stood there, a scowl drawing his brows together. Age had finally begun to mark his face. His jaw had begun to sag, and deep lines fanned from the corners of his eyes. All the time he spent on the golf course, maybe. His expression was a mixture of boredom and irritation, and for half a second Sam toyed with the idea of just letting the door close again, but he wasn't going to act like a shit-brick who didn't finish what he started.

He stepped off the elevator.

"Your brother's in my office waiting."

His tone triggered Sam's temper. He gritted his teeth and bit back a comment. "I'm not here to see you or Trevor. I'm here to see Tim."

"You can take a few minutes to apologize to your brother."

"I don't have anything to apologize for."

Thomas's glance conveyed all the disgust it usually did when

Sam refused to toe the line. Sam smiled.

He followed his father down the hall and into his office.

The skin beneath Trevor's eyes was faintly green from the broken nose of two weeks past, his expression reminiscent of his childhood sulks. Some things never changed.

"I don't have time to be a referee or act as an arbiter between you two," Thomas said.

Not surprising, since he never had time for them any other time, either. "It won't be necessary. What I'd have to say wouldn't take two minutes."

Thomas raised a brow.

Sam turned his attention to Trevor. "I want to know what the problem is between us, Trev. You've been a real fucker toward me since you passed the bar and started working here."

His father's brows rose. "Is that directed at me?"

"Why? Do you feel responsible for it?"

"I hired him because he's a good lawyer. Just like you would have been."

"I wouldn't have made it a day here. I'd have punched you in the face just like I did him." He turned his attention back to Trevor. "I can take care of myself. But you went after Moira like she was a criminal... Why would you do that?"

Trevor tucked his hands into his pockets. "It wasn't one of my finest moments. But costing me my girlfriend was perfect payback wasn't it?"

"Based on what Paige said, I'd say she was already halfway out the door, and you were hoping a diamond on her finger would swing the deal."

Trevor's face flushed bright red. "You're a son of a bitch. If you were any kind of brother you'd be on my side."

"You treated Paige like shit, Trevor, and you know it. And then you started in on Moira. Someone you'd never met. What the hell, Trev? Why would you go after her?"

"Your hard-headed sanctimonious bullshit is getting old, Sam. It cost us when we were kids, and it's still costing us. Mom still thinks the sun rises and sets in you, and you ignore her and the rest of us."

He'd had enough of this blame game. "I don't ignore Mom, I just make sure to go see her when you're not around, because of this kind of bullshit. I didn't call Thomas up on the phone and tell him not to show up for visitation. I didn't do anything to keep him from pursuing a relationship with you and Tim. He made that decision on his own. So if you're going to point a finger, direct it at the guy responsible." Sam pointed a thumb back at his father.

"You can leave me out of this, Samuel."

Thomas's tone enraged him every time.

"Like you left us out of your life for years. Own up to your own shit, you cowardly fucker. I'm tired of being blamed for your failures and carrying the emotional wreckage you leave behind." He was done with this shit. He focused on Trevor. "And if you don't realize that it's his responsibility, not mine, then I'm sorry for you, Trevor." He strode toward the door.

"You're really good at walking away instead of holding your ground, aren't you Samuel?"

"I hold my ground just fine when it really counts, old man. You're the one who fucked up here. Not me. If you'd given one shit about any of us, at least more than your dick, Trevor and Tim wouldn't still be carrying this. Deal with it or not. But it isn't on me anymore."

He glanced at Trevor. "Why do you think he paid for college for all of us, while insisting we all become lawyers? Why do you think he wanted you to follow in his footsteps? Because he's a selfish, narcissistic asshole, and he's encouraging you to be the same, Trevor. You're not a kid anymore, and you don't need to put up with his shit to earn his approval. An approval you'll never get. Get a clue. Or stay the fuck away from me."

He stalked out of the room and down the hall. There was no healing this breach. Not until his father grew a pair and owned up to it. And it would never happen. He'd continue to look out for himself always and to hell with everyone else.

And Trevor would have to eventually get smart when Thomas threw him under the bus for something and cost him more than he was willing to pay.

"Sam." Tim rushed toward him. "What the hell happened?"

"Dad ambushed me before as I stepped off the elevator."

"Shit! I'm sorry. Come back to my office before he starts something else."

He'd never felt less like sticking around anywhere, but it was his little brother asking. Tim's office looked like a closet compared to Trevor's, but his desk was impressive.

"What's going on?" he asked as soon as he shut the door.

"I applied for a job at another firm, and I've been hired. I'll be leaving at the end of the day."

Tim was so quiet and laid back that it was always a shock when he did something unexpected. "When did you apply?"

"A couple of weeks ago." He sat down behind the desk and Sam took one of the visitor's chairs.

"You're right about Trevor, and you've always been right about Dad. The idea of Dad has always been better than the real deal, but Trevor just can't give up the dream. He wants to follow in Dad's footsteps. He wants to be his right-hand man, and he is, because there's nothing he won't do to please him. But Dad still doesn't have anything to do with us outside of the business. It's just not in him to be a father."

He picked up a globe-shaped paperweight and rolled it be-tween his hands. "You were more of a father to us than Dad ever was. Teaching us how to play ball, helping us with our homework. You were just a kid yourself, and you just jumped in to fill the gaps. Trevor knows it. We've even talked about it.

"But after the other day at Mom's house... Plus there were a couple of things that happened here that I couldn't turn a blind eye to... I can't even be in the room with Dad anymore. I'm tired of the way he tries to manipulate us both. Tired of watching Trevor allow him to manipulate him. He still needs him. I don't."

He wasn't tortured by their father's rejection like Trevor. Why? Maybe those few years in age made the difference. Sam drew a deep breath. "Any suggestions for how we can help Trevor put Thomas behind him?"

"He's not a kid anymore, Sam. The choices he makes are his own."

"Dad will throw him under the bus sooner or later. And there won't be a damn thing we can do about it."

Tim's expression was grave. "When it happens, we'll be there to help him. Until then there isn't a damn thing we can do."

He had to accept that and move on. "Can I help you pack?"

Tim laughed. "Sure. And deliver some boxes to my new office. I don't have room in my car for everything."

"Where will you be working?" Sam asked.

"The DA's office."

Sam kept his jaw from dropping—barely.

"You know I clerked for Judge Carter. And I did more work in criminal law than I did in business. I had a whole group of professors who wrote me letters of reference so I wouldn't have to ask Dad for a job. He'd have trashed me out of spite."

He would have. And what did that say about the man who fathered them? "I hope it's something you can be passionate about, Tim."

He grinned. "It is. I always have been."

God, he looked so young. And he hated to see Tim's idealism stamped out by the seamier side of things he'd inevitably have to deal with in the DA's office, but if it was what he wanted…

As a new kid on the block, Tim wouldn't be working on the Mark Travis or Denise Clayborn cases, something to be grateful for.

And was fucked up, too. He couldn't ask his brother questions about either case any more than Tim could ask him questions about where he'd been and what he'd done when he was deployed. The whole family seemed destined to work in fields that required confidentiality. Damn it.

"Since you'll be working there, I guess you should know I was at the Del the night Mark Travis was killed. And I sat at the dinner table that night with Denise and Nelson Clayborn."

"And she was killed two weeks after Mark," Tim added. "Have the police talked to you about Denise's shooting?"

"No. But they did about Mark's death. They talked to everyone who was there that night. Moira found his body."

Tim's brows rose. "Jesus! How did that happen?"

"After I left, she went out on the balcony and saw him on the ground below. She thought it was someone passed out. When she realized he was dead, she called the police. He'd been dead a while."

"Is she okay?" Tim asked.

Leave it to his little brother to realize what a trauma it was for her. "She's had a few nightmares since then. But she's doing okay."

"And since Trevor pulled that bullshit at Mom's?"

"I thought she'd walk away and wash her hands of me, but she didn't. She certainly doesn't want to ever see Trevor again."

"Understandable. I'll be relieved to have some distance myself from him and Dad both."

Tim should have never come to work for Thomas. He'd wasted a year of his life here.

Sam stood. "Where are those boxes, and where do you need them delivered?"

Tim grinned and reached for a pad and pen. "I'll write the address down for you. My office there is only a little bigger than this one, but I'll be doing work that matters."

"I'm happy for you, bro."

"I hope you're happy enough not to mind the two tons of stuff I need to move. And you might want to move your car to the back alley so we can load it." Tim pulled open the door to a small closet. Inside were boxes stacked to the ceiling. "They're heavy—it's mostly books and my diplomas."

Shit. Two tons of shit in a closet-sized office. "I'll mosey on down the back stairs and move the car."

"Thanks, Sam."

"No problem. I hope you have a dolly, too."

"By the time you get back with the car, I will."

Sam paused by the office door before opening it. "Dad won't let you walk away quietly."

Tim's expression hardened and he suddenly looked older. "Yes, he will. I know where the dirt is. He causes me any shit, I'll make certain the right people get that information. No matter who I work for, I'm still an officer of the court."

Jesus! Who'd have thought his little brother could play hardball with Thomas Harding?

Sam grabbed Tim and gave him a hard hug. "I'll get the car."

CHAPTER 13

MOIRA TOOK A step back from the canvas to study the value from light to dark of the woman's red hair. It was good, but she needed to add some highlights here and there to make the flow of her hair have a little movement.

A knock on the door cut off her debate about exactly where she would place those highlights. She dropped her brush in water and crossing the room, shut the door behind her.

She didn't want Sam to see the painting. Not yet. But keeping it a secret had been difficult. He'd been at her apartment as much as he'd been at his own. He even left what he called a go bag in her closet and a toothbrush and a shaving kit in her bathroom.

If she offered him a key, would it make him feel like she was pushing for more too quickly? And she would be. Was she ready to offer him a key? Maybe. Maybe not. He was wary of taking a step toward anything permanent.

Was she? Was that where she hoped their relationship was going?

It had only been four weeks. Four weeks that had seemed like so much longer. They were a couple. At least she thought they were. He was always so careful not to say anything about feelings, but sometimes when he looked at her....

She was already certain of how she felt. She loved him. Loved every moment they were together. If he walked away tomorrow, she'd still love him.

And knowing it was exciting, and wonderful, and terrifying, all at the same time.

She tried not to dwell on it, or the fact that he could be deployed at a moment's notice, despite being involved in training a SEAL class.

She opened the door. It wasn't Sam. For a second she stood stock still.

Elizabeth Travis's son stood head and shoulders taller than she was, and his expressive eyes and dark brown hair suited his narrow face, much handsomer than his father's.

She managed a, "Hello."

"Ms. McKee, I'm Michael Travis. We met at the charity benefit a month ago."

"Yes, I remember you. Please come in." She stepped back to allow him to come inside, then shut the door.

"My mom asked me to drop off this paperwork for you to fill out for human resources. There are some pictures in there of her and Sarah and the rest of our family." He extended a manila envelope, and she automatically accepted it from him.

"Thank you for bringing them to me. I'll fill out the paperwork and drop it by the office." She laid the envelope on the end table closest to her.

"Mom said you were going to fill in for Luisa for a couple of weeks."

"Just long enough for your mom to settle on someone who'll take over the position permanently. Mostly I'll be painting the mural your mother wants for the lobby."

He nodded. "Mom said you're an artist and a teacher."

"Yes, high school art."

"Why did you choose to raise money for my mom's charity when you could have raised it to fund art in schools or education?"

"My school was looking for a local service project to take on. My youngest brother, Kyle, was premature, and had the NICU staff not worked with us and kept him going, we'd have lost him.

So when I read that your mother's charity was raising money to build a new NICU unit, I thought I'd go to my school and encourage them to use the fundraiser as a community project where the whole school could get involved."

"I understand why my mom wants you to work with her. You have the same obsession she does."

His tone held a hint of resentment. She could understand. It had to be hard to compete with a nonprofit organization inspired by a sibling who died before Michael was born.

How difficult had it been to have a mother obsessed with a dead child and a father obsessed with sleeping with every woman who crossed his path?

Had anyone put Michael first?

"I think your mother, through her charity, has helped a lot of people avoid some of the heartbreak she experienced. She's certainly given back to the community."

"I think she's done enough. I'd like to see her do something else. She's been having a hard time since Dad died. She's been distracted, and spends a lot of time driving around in her car."

"She's grieving in her way, just as you're grieving in yours."

His eyes darted away. "She said you found my dad."

Why had Elizabeth told him? That wasn't something she'd think a mother would share with her child. "Yes, I did." When he seemed to want her to go on, she bit her lip. "I think it was sudden and unexpected. And I don't think he suffered."

"Had you ever met him before?"

"Your mother introduced me to him at the dinner just before she had to go onstage. We just said, nice to meet you, and I went back to my seat. I'm so sorry you and your mother have lost him. I know it's very painful."

Michael shifted his shoulders. "Our senior prom was that night. I swung by the hotel since Mom wanted to take pictures of me and my girlfriend before we went to the dance. We were late getting to school because of it."

"Did you have a good time?"

He looked up. "Yeah." He forked his fingers through his hair while pain flickered across his young face. "My dad was dying while I was partying."

"You were doing what all teenagers do during and after prom. You were living the moment. Your dad wouldn't have minded that, Michael."

He was silent for a moment. "Maybe. He liked to party, too."

There was an undertone in his voice she couldn't read, and he didn't meet her eyes. Had he known about the many women his father *partied* with?

His head came up suddenly. "I gotta go. You can fax the form to the office. The number is on the bottom of the first page. It'll save you a trip."

"Thanks, I'll do that." She walked him back to the door and opened it.

Sam stood outside in the hall. "Hey."

His gaze traveled to Michael standing next to her.

"Sam, do you know Michael Travis?"

"No, but I'm acquainted with your mom and dad." Sam offered his hand, and Michael accepted it and shook. "I'm sorry about your father, Michael."

"Thanks. I saw you at the fundraiser, didn't I?"

"Yes. I was there dancing with Moira."

Michael smiled for the first time. "The food sucks and the only good things about those shindigs are the music and dancing."

Sam grinned. "Agreed. Tell your mom Sam Harding sends his best."

"Will do." He threw up a hand. "Bye, Ms. McKee." The man-boy sauntered on down the hall in the direction of the elevator.

"What was that about?"

"He was dropping off some paperwork and pictures from his mother. I'm working up a drawing for the lobby painting." She didn't want to tell him she'd accepted the two-week job.

"How was Book?" she asked.

He shook his head. "Not great." He hunched his shoulders in a way that telegraphed he didn't want to talk about it. "I also went by to see Tim. He's accepted a job in the DA's office and is moving there. I helped him transport some stuff to his new office."

She couldn't imagine the mild-mannered man who'd served her ice water at their mother's house prosecuting criminals. "The DA's office?"

"Yeah. It blew me away, too. I'm so fucking proud of him."

She laughed. "Yeah, it's hard to take in. Can Tim handle it?"

"He's sharp and he's tougher than he looks. He'd have to be to survive a year in practice with Thomas. But he surprised me with this move."

"I wonder what your mom thinks about it."

"She'll be relieved he's out from under Thomas's thumb."

She was troubled by his obvious dislike of his father. "Is your dad really as bad as you keep saying he is?"

Sam focused on her. "You saw Trevor in action. He learned all that from Dad. Multiply it by ten and you'll have Thomas Harding. He's relentless. And cruel."

The mention of Trevor was enough. She couldn't imagine having to fend off attacks from her family members, and was glad she'd never met him. "I'm so grateful for my parents. They're always supportive. I know your mom has always been too."

"I already know how yours are. They raised you."

Her breath caught. "You'd be open to meeting them if they come to visit?"

His caramel colored gaze flashed to her. "Why would you think I wouldn't be?"

"I thought you might be a little uneasy about it. My parents are very curious. They ask me about you all the time."

"What have you told them?"

"Just that you're in the Navy. And that you're *very* affectionate." She bit her bottom lip to keep from smiling.

His tawny gaze settled on her face. "Affectionate huh? You know that's code for I'm having sex with your daughter. The whole time I'm talking to your dad or your brothers, they'll be thinking of new and different ways they can bury my body in the desert."

She laughed, relieved to know he was open to meeting her family. She slipped an arm around his waist and cuddled up. "I promise I'll protect you."

His arms tightened around her, and he brushed her forehead with his lips.

Guilt was like a bothersome itch. She needed to tell him about the two-week gig she'd signed on for.

"Let's go out," he suggested. There was a tension in him she'd seen before after his visits to Book, but today he seemed even more worked up.

Relieved at the suggestion, she said, "I need to change." She gestured to her loose top and leggings.

"You'll want to put on something warmer. I thought we'd pick up something to eat and take the boat out for a little while. We could even spend the night if you want. You don't have anything scheduled for tomorrow, do you?"

"No. It's Sunday. I was planning to be lazy all day."

"You're never lazy. You always have something going on."

She did most of the time. "Not tomorrow."

He drew her in close and kissed her while he stroked her ass. "We'll be lazy together."

Feeling the change in his body, she said, "You don't feel very lazy."

Sam laughed.

She had never engaged in suggestive wordplay before. There were so many new things she was experiencing with him. Things she hadn't allowed herself to experience because of her weight and the trauma of that first experience. The way his body reacted to hers was one of them.

Sam could be romantic, moody, and intense, all at once...like now.

"Go get changed." He patted her ass. "We'll pick up provisions."

"Okay." She reached for the envelope on the way to her room. She paused before entering the hall and looked back at him. "What else happened today besides seeing Book and Tim?"

"We'll talk about it later."

She started to offer support, but his closed expression made her wary. She continued on down the hall to change.

THE BRINY SCENT of the sea and the roll and slap of the waves against the hull as they motored out of the dock area soothed the edgy feeling that stuck with Sam like a burr.

He hadn't been able to shake off the argument earlier in the day. It was frustrating as hell watching while Trevor turned into Thomas. He was like a puppy wagging its tail, wanting attention, but instead of a pat on the head, he got a boot up the ass. It was exactly what Thomas wanted, and Trevor would end up being humiliated and undermined the entire time he was working for their father.

Or he'd be pushed to do things illegal, immoral, or unethical.

And that was what was eating at Sam. There wasn't a damn thing he could do about it. Dammit!

He shifted his focus to Moira as she stood at the railing. She was giving him space, somehow always seeming to know when he needed it. He prided himself on not showing his feelings, but she could read him like a book. Too bad he couldn't read her as easily.

But he could see there was something going on with her. She'd been quiet. He was noticing things more and more. Since she'd told him about her weight issue, he'd noticed how careful she was about what and how much she ate. She was religious about her swimming. He'd gone with her a couple of times, and was impressed with how strong a swimmer she was.

Although he hadn't yet gone with her to the hospital to watch her cuddle the babies. That just seemed...too close for comfort. He wasn't ready...not yet.

He turned the boat south and headed for a cove where he'd put in several times. Moira left the rail and strolled over to him, slipping her arms around him from behind. Her breasts nestled in against him, and she rested her cheek against his spine between his shoulder blades. He was hard and ready for her in an instant.

She slipped away before he could turn and draw her in.

"Thank you for suggesting this. I needed it," she said.

"I did too."

"What do you do to decompress when you're deployed?" she asked.

"Lift weights, play ball, whatever physical training I can do."

"This is much better, isn't it?"

"Yeah it is. Sometimes I meditate. Don't tell any of the guys that, because I'll have to deny it."

She grinned. "Not macho enough?"

"Something like that."

"I think whatever helps you get through things is good."

Sam slipped an arm around her and tucked her against his side. Was sex on that list? He eased the boat starboard to cross over the wake of a smaller vessel racing down the coastline.

"You've helped me get past some major hurdles since we've been dating."

And what was he supposed to say to that? Damn, it was hard to share when you felt like a wuss when you did it. "I've never been as open with anyone I've dated as I am with you."

She rested her head against his shoulder. "And it only hurt a little for you to say that, huh?"

Her wry humor always got him, and he chuckled. "Since we're sharing, there's something I've wanted to know for a few weeks now."

"What?"

"What did your roommates say about your hair?"

She was silent for a long moment. "They called me Bush. Hey, Bush, have you combed today? Hey, Bush, you might need a trim, but a wax might be better. Like a joke, but it wasn't."

The cruelty of it sent a sharp, hard thrust of rage through him, so intense he couldn't speak for a moment. "It was your hair that first caught my attention and drew me to you, Moira. It's beautiful, and has a life of its own."

He wrapped a strand around his finger, then withdrew it, creating a corkscrew curl that dangled against her cheek. "You're right to forget about those…" He swallowed against the need to call them something foul. "…women. They're not worth remembering. And if karma is a thing, everything they did has come back around to bite them." And he hoped every bite drew blood.

He guided the boat into the cove and put the engine in neutral. "I need to set the anchor so we won't drift into shore."

"I can help."

"Okay. Toss out the anchor. It's on the starboard side of the deck. I'll put the Gypsy in reverse and drag the anchor until it's set and will hold us in place."

"Okay." She was picking up skills and was eager to help. None of the other women he'd had on the boat had shown an interest. Or was it because he hadn't trusted them enough to allow them to do things to help?

He put the boat in reverse, set the anchor, then turned off the engine. He moved forward and watched Moira crank the anchor chain so the boat wouldn't move. "That's good enough. You need about six feet of slack so the boat's movements won't tear the anchor loose and drag it."

What made Moira different from the other women he'd dated?

He felt a deeper connection to her, had from the start. Or had he just been more open to her after his mother put the idea in his head?

Idea or not, it was Moira who'd drawn him physically. With her wry sense of humor and her shy sensuality, she'd been sexy as hell and hadn't even known it. That's what hooked him that first night, and continued to do so.

He caught her hand and tugged her toward the cabin.

"Are you that hungry?"

"Yeah, but not for food."

A look of surprise and pleasure leaped into her eyes, and she smiled. He was hard as stone in a second. He lifted her down the steps while his mouth covered hers. Her avid response shot another bolt of lust straight to his groin.

He bent and lifted her so she straddled his hips and looped her legs around him. In two strides he reached the galley table and sat her on the edge. His hands shaking, he tugged her sweatshirt up and over her head and tossed it on one of the bench seats, and her bra soon followed. He eased her down on the table and lowered his mouth to her breast, suckling one peach-colored nipple while he worked the zipper of her jeans down, thrust his hand down her pants, and found her hot and wet as he thrust one finger inside her and Moira cried out, her hips undulating with her climax.

God, she was good for his ego. She was so sensitive and so easy to get off.

She was still recovering when he peeled her pants and panties off and dropped his pants. "Put your legs over my arms." Sam grasped the edge of the table, and as soon as she did what he asked, he thrust inside her. Her body gripped him with moist heat, and he almost climaxed immediately, but fought it back. He leaned over her and pumped in and out with short, quick movements, pushing into her as far as he could.

The pleasure built to a sharp peak, until a fierce, consuming release roared through him like a missile. He buried his face against Moira's neck and gasped for air like a beached fish while he breathed in the sweet, floral fragrance that clung to her skin.

Moira's hand stroked the back of his neck. His legs shook. Sweet Jesus! He'd never known anything like this. By now his hunger for her should have diminished. But it hadn't.

He eased out of her and looked down at his flaccid dick. Dammit! He'd forgotten the condom. He wasn't worried about disease. But the idea of pregnancy was a little concerning. Actually, a lot concerning. He fought back the rush of panic.

CHAPTER 14

MOIRA SAT UP and tried to read his expression. As soon as he entered her she'd known, but it had felt so wonderful to be skin-to-skin with nothing between them. Was he freaking out? He was so hard to read.

He tucked everything away and hiked his pants back in place before his tawny gaze fastened on her.

A breeze whipped down the steps, chilling her, and she crossed her arms over her breasts.

Sam picked up her bra and held it for her to slip into and hooked it. Next came the panties discarded on the deck. He helped her dress, one piece of clothing at a time, his hands smoothing her top into place, his fingers nimbly fastening the top button of her jeans and tugging up the zipper. There was a patient care in everything he did that took her breath away.

When she was wearing all but her shoes, he leaned down and kissed her softly. She felt the brush of his mouth against hers from her lips to the soles of her feet.

"I'm clean, and I know you are," he said.

"Yes."

"Are you on birth control?"

"Yes."

It was impossible to read his reaction.

He moved in close and leaned down to take her lips again. His breath fanned her ear as he whispered, "It felt fantastic being inside you without a condom." She shivered, and a renewed ache of arousal settled down low.

"Let's eat."

She laughed. "I may not be able to look at that table again without thinking about what we just did on it. We may want to clean it before we eat on it."

He chuckled, his expression free of the tension that had worried her earlier. "I'll do that, but I thought we might want to eat up on deck."

It took only a few minutes to clean up and gather the sandwiches and drinks they'd picked up on the way. "Here. I'll carry the drinks," Sam offered and grasped them by hooking the tops of the bottles between his fingers.

Moira climbed the steps, and hearing a Jet Ski coming toward them from the bay, she looked up. A rider in a black wet suit appeared, heading straight toward them. He seemed to throw up a hand in a wave, and she half raised her hand to return the greeting.

A dull pop sounded, a hole appeared in the wood trim around the door leading down into the cabin, and splinters flew. Another pop sounded, Sam dove toward her, knocking her down, then crawled forward and covered her with his body. "Jesus Christ. He's shooting at us." The Jet Ski whined as it flew past, its wake rocking the boat.

"Hug the deck and get back downstairs."

He didn't have to tell her twice. She half-crawled, half-fell down the steps, with Sam close behind her.

He rushed to a cabinet over the tiny galley stove, withdrew a pistol, and a slapped a clip into it like she'd seen cops do on television. Intent, he strode toward the door.

Fear for him had her heart rate skyrocketing. Moira stepped in his path, blocking him. "Don't go up there, Sam." The whine of the watercraft engine revved again, and the boat rocked gently. "Please."

With one last whine, the sound outside grew distant then faded.

"He's gone." Sam's arm went around her, and he nestled her against him. She clung to him as quick tears stung her eyes. She fought them back.

"We have to notify the Coast Guard," he said.

She nodded.

While she watched him at the radio, she saw the soldier in action, his voice clipped, succinct, and all business. He'd remained so calm during the entire episode, it made those moments seem surreal.

But eventually what happened began to sink in. At first she had no idea she was being shot at, then she was frozen by shock. He'd knocked her down and put himself between her and the threat, and he'd been prepared to face the shooter.

She sank down into the bench at the table, her legs going weak with reaction.

"You okay?" Sam asked.

Though she was more than a little shaky, she nodded. "I didn't see the gun. He was wearing a black wet suit and the gun was black and blended in."

"I know."

"You saved my life, Sam."

He squatted down in front of her and rested a hand on her knee. "The chances that he could have hit either one of us while riding a ski jet and firing a pistol would have been astronomical. That crap only happens in the movies."

"He got close, and he could have gotten lucky."

"But he didn't. And that's all that counts."

How many times had he been shot at that he could shrug it aside so easily?

"The Coast Guard will be here in a few minutes to assess the scene and write up their report. They'll notify the San Diego police, and they'll want to interview us both, too. In the meantime I want you to think about a few things. Have you noticed anybody following you to or from school? Or have you gotten the feeling that someone is watching you?"

"No. But then I haven't been looking for anyone."

"Have you had any kind of run-in with a student recently?"

"No. We're gearing down at school, and everyone is more than ready to finish and be out for summer break. The students are being pretty cooperative, probably partly because Mr. Jacobs has the concert to hold over their heads. They cause an issue and they don't get to attend. What are you thinking?"

"Since Denise was killed and your car was doused with paint…and now this…I'm starting to think something more may be going on."

"There isn't any reason for anyone to want to hurt me, Sam. I haven't done anything to make anyone angry or to trigger an attack."

"You may not even be aware of what you might have done or said. If this person is crazy…"

The bullets hadn't been flying just at her. "Is there anyone who might be after you? The man was shooting at you too."

He remained silent for a long moment. "There could be any number of governments who might like to hunt me down if they knew who I am, Moira. That's why we don't permit pictures or allow anyone to publish anything about us. It would be like painting a target on our backs."

She nodded. "Maybe it was just a random thing. Maybe he thought he could steal the boat if he managed to kill us. We're anchored here in a secluded place. And the boat is worth a lot of money."

"That's true enough. Had he come a few minutes earlier…"

The sound of a large engine approaching grew loud and the Gypsy rocked as it pulled alongside. "Ahoy, Gypsy. this is the Coast Guard cutter Endurance."

"We have to go topside, Moira. Think about what I said." He offered his hand, and she took it.

CHAPTER 15

MOIRA STOOD BY the wide gates watching the crowd file out of the football field. It had been a beautiful, clear day with a steady breeze offsetting the seventy-five-degree heat. Ticket sales had surprised even her, because they almost sold out. And there were zero incidents of bad behavior by students or attendees, for which she was extremely grateful.

It had taken some haggling with the board and the city to get a temporary permit for such a large event, and to add the extra food, drink, and security. But it had all gone off without a hitch. Well, with just a few tiny hitches.

Relief was all she could feel at the moment. The pressure on her to make sure everything went smoothly was still riding her shoulders. How the hell had she ended up being pushed into doing the lion's share of the work *again*?

Sam was right about one thing. She had set up her program to be a failure for anyone who followed her. And she had set things up so her principal was leaning on her more and more for big-ticket items that drained her reserves. The next thing that came up, she would say no. She had to.

She'd set up a cleaning crew from the sports teams to gather any extra trash left behind. The bleachers rental place was already at the gate with a truck, waiting until the last few people exited so they could load the bleachers in time to deliver them to the next venue.

Students were already swarming the field, eager to get things squared away so they could go home. All of that was on Mr. Jacobs' shoulders, not hers.

Thank God. She was eager to leave. She'd have the summer break to recuperate. Once the students left, she wouldn't see them again until the first day of school in the fall.

Sam appeared at the gate with Bullet, Gilly, and the new team member, Simon Beckham. T-shirts stretched across their broad shoulders, and printed with the word Security across their chests, showed off their well-toned, muscular physiques.

She owed Sam big time. He'd talked his team into being security for the entire event free of charge. But she had something special for them in her car as a thank-you. Something she'd needed to plot and maneuver to make sure Sam hadn't seen it yet.

The men wandered over to the vehicle and leaned against it in identical poses, ankles and arms crossed.

"Were there any problems?" she asked.

"Nah," Bullet replied. "People were enjoying the music and having a good time. Piece of cake."

"Where are the others?"

"We flipped coins. They're rounding up stragglers and making sure the bathrooms are empty," Sam said. "They'll be along soon."

Shy of touching him in front of his men, Moira settled back against the left front quarter panel next to him to wait, and smiled when he put an arm around her and encouraged her to lean against him.

"Have you ever thought about going into the Navy, Moira?" Simon asked.

"No. Why?"

"You'd be great in operations. You seem to have a flair for organizing the troops and getting stuff done."

"And wading through red tape," Sam added.

Moira laughed. "Thanks. But no. Military service isn't for me. I know my physical and mental limitations, but I sure admire you guys for being able to work past yours."

Sam gave her a squeeze. "She's serving in a different way. Moira's been going by to see Book with me. She's actually got him painting."

"No, shit?" Gilly exclaimed, brows raised.

She shrugged. "He's taking his aggressions and grief and putting them on canvas."

Bullet leaned away from the car to look around Sam. "I know some other guys who could use that. You might have a new career."

She'd thought the same after she started working with Book, with his doctor's and the hospital therapist's blessing. But going back to school for an art therapy degree seemed daunting.

With each new person in Sam's life she became involved with, she felt closer to him. But worry niggled at her too. What if he and the others deployed, leaving her here alone? She'd miss them all, grieve for them all.

None of them were married. Some had girlfriends, but they all seemed to avoid commitment. Why was that? Didn't they need someone here to give them support?

Squirrel, Swan, Denotti, and Arrow appeared from behind the stands, walking behind a group of six people.

"A few big fans just hanging around hoping for an autograph," Denotti explained as they reached the car.

"I have something for you guys as a thank-you for helping out tonight. Actually, two somethings. One is serious, and one isn't.

She moved around the car to open the trunk. She removed a framed picture and handed it to Denotti. "You said you wanted a bombshell."

The motorcycle's chrome motor and fenders glinted in the sun. Walking toward it was a voluptuous redhead wearing black leather, a motorcycle helmet held against her hip. She was paused in mid-step and glancing over her shoulder at the viewer, a sexy invitation in her eyes.

The guys clustered around the painting. None said actual words, but each seemed to make sounds of admiration.

"Ooo, baby!" Gilly murmured.

The rest laughed. Denotti's grin was white against the scruff of his beard. "She'll do."

"I'm glad you're pleased. I have prints for each of you, as well as one each of this."

She reached in the trunk again and tore away the bubble wrap covering the frame.

Book and Beck stood together in the midst of all the others. The men leaned against each other like they'd paused for a photo as a team. They were all in combat gear, but they slouched in the way men had when they were completely at ease with one another.

"I hope I got everything right," she said when they remained silent.

"Has Book seen this?" Sam asked.

"No, not yet."

"Don't show it to him until he's in a better place."

"I won't. But I couldn't leave him out."

He nodded. "Understood." He continued to study the drawing. "It's damn fine, Moira." The emotion in his gaze gripped her throat and her eyes stung.

"We'll hang it in the cage, guys."

Denotti still held the painting. "And her?"

Sam grinned. "We'll hang her where every one of us can pat her fine, fine ass for luck every time we go out."

Their masculine laughter eased the serious mood, and when the group broke up to get into their vehicles, they were all still grinning.

Beck paused beside Moira on his way to his motorcycle. His auburn hair lay thick across his forehead, and his pale blue eyes were startling in his ruddy face, "Thanks for including me."

"You're one of the team. Thanks for helping with security."

"No problem." When he offered his hand, she bumped knuckles with him. For a moment she felt like one of the guys, until she turned to Sam and saw the look in his eyes.

ONCE INSIDE THE car. Sam searched for the right words to thank her. "That was… You're a class act, Moira."

She smiled. "I promised them a painting."

"She's a beauty. The guys will get a lot of mileage out of her, but the other one, they'll carry that one forever."

"That's why I love what I do."

"And you'll have the summer to paint as much as you want."

"Well, actually… I won't…. I've been offered a temporary job for part of the summer."

What the hell? She'd been looking forward to having time to decompress and paint. "What kind of temporary job?"

"Elizabeth Travis wants me to be her personal assistant for two or three weeks until she finishes interviews for the position, but I've told her I can't. But I did tell her I would work with her team and show them step by step how we set up the process of fundraising at school, and I'm going to be doing the painting for the lobby at her office."

He remained silent for a moment. She'd referred to it before, but after the shooting on the Gypsy he thought she'd drop it. He didn't like the idea of her being mixed up with the Travis's business.

"So, you'd be a creative consultant?"

"That's how she described it."

"They still haven't discovered who's responsible for Mark Travis or Denise Clayborn's murders. Or who shot at us while we were on the boat."

"We don't know if Mark Travis was killed or if it was an accident, and there's never been any connection mentioned between the two deaths. And we can't assume the shooter at the boat had any connection either.

"You don't really think I'd be in danger at their offices, do you? I'll be there with other people. No one has a motive for hurting me. I barely know Elizabeth, and I only met her husband for about thirty seconds."

"No one had motive to pour paint on your car, either, or shoot at us."

"The police think the paint thing was kids, Sam."

"I don't want you taking any chances, Moira."

Her checks pinkened. "I've already told her I'd meet with her team and do the painting. They've set aside room for me already, and purchased the canvas."

"You can move the canvas to your studio at home."

"I don't have room for it, Sam. It's about twelve feet long and six feet wide."

"Why so big?"

"They're going to hang it above the lobby so it's seen by everyone who walks into the building. It's a progression of what her daughter would have looked like at different times of her life. It will stretch the length of the lobby. I'll show you the pastel I did as an example."

Jesus! She was too good at what she did. Too talented to be teaching school when there were so many other things she could do. But she made decisions with her heart instead of her head. And threw herself into things without thinking it through. He was all about analyzing the situation and working the problem.

"I don't want you to do it. I'd like you to give the cops time to find out what happened before you start hanging with Elizabeth."

"I've already given her my word, Sam."

And Moira didn't break her word. She'd bend over backwards and sideways before it happened. And she'd let people take advantage of her before she finally said no.

"Why didn't you mention this to me before?"

"I've been busy with the concert planning, and I kept putting off a decision. I really look forward to my breaks, because once school is back in session it's nonstop activity."

"And you let your principal railroad you into dealing with all the stuff that went with hosting a concert."

"Yeah, I did. But I'm putting my foot down, I'm not doing it anymore."

Yes, she would.

He started the car but didn't put it in gear.

"You don't believe me, do you?" Her tone was part accusing,

part fact.

"No." He hadn't meant to be so abrupt, but the more he thought about her being in Elizabeth Travis's offices… He had a bad feeling about all of it.

And the police believed Travis had been murdered. Otherwise they wouldn't have been going all out with a full-fledged investigation, and the news stations wouldn't have continued to cover the story off and on.

He turned off the car and rested his elbow on the steering wheel. "You didn't let me talk you into anything that first night we met, did you?"

"No, of course not."

"But you let your principal and Elizabeth talk you into things you don't want to do."

"It's different. With my principal, he's my boss, and I have to do what he asks if I want to keep my job. With Elizabeth, it was a business decision. If I didn't do the painting, I would be losing out on the opportunity to get my work out before a very wide audience. With you…it was personal."

That interested him enough to distract him from the argument that was brewing. "You asked me to come back when I called to check on you. Why did you do that?"

She remained silent for nearly thirty seconds, her face averted. "Every time you touched me, I wanted you. I'd never experienced that with anyone else."

"Not even the guy you were with before?"

She flinched. "We weren't really together. I'd gone out with him a couple of times. Just to eat and to a ball game. The third time we went out was to a party." She seemed to brace herself. "I wish I could say I was young and drunk and don't remember any of it. But I was twenty, lonely, and he was the first guy who'd shown any interest in me. I remember everything."

She closed her eyes, and a flicker of pain flashed over her lovely face. "When he didn't call me for a week afterwards, I ran into him on campus and asked him why."

Silence stretched as she grappled with her composure. Sam

gripped the steering wheel until his hands ached, wanting to demand the guy's name so he could find the son of a bitch and beat the shit out of him.

"I was different then. Shy, quiet, and sixty pounds heavier than I am now."

He struggled to wrap his head around that. Her body was toned and fit. He'd touched every inch of her, and aside from a few stretchmarks on her breasts and on the sides of her hips...

"I won't repeat what he said to me. But I didn't go on another date for nearly two years, and I never got close to any of the guys I dated. We'd go out for a meal or sports events, a movie. I suppose part of the reason guys dumped me wasn't because I was over-weight, but because I didn't want to have sex with them."

That caught his attention.

"I had no confidence in the way I looked. And then the experience in college... I didn't really trust any of them."

He cleared his throat. "But you trusted me?"

"Yes. I'd lost the weight, and I'd worked hard to get past my self-image issues. I felt ready to move forward from that first horrible experience. And after you left, I regretted not inviting you up. I didn't know if I'd ever again feel for anyone like I did with you." She twisted the hem of her T-shirt into a knot, drawing it tight around her.

Just listening to her talk about her feelings for him made him hard as steel. Was she getting in too deep with him? And was he getting in too deep with her? Surprised he wasn't feeling the panic he usually did when the current woman he was with became too involved, he reached for her hand.

"Men can't really hide their physical feelings the way women can, Moira. I'm sure you were aware of my attraction to you from the moment we danced and kissed. I wanted you the moment I saw you standing next to the table with your flame-colored hair and perfect, pale skin."

"Not perfect."

"Close enough. None of us are perfect. Perfect is for sculp-tures, not real human beings."

"I know. I never wanted perfection. I just wanted someone to look at me like you did that night. Like you do while we make love."

He grew painfully hard. "Do you have pictures of yourself before you lost the weight?"

"Yes."

"When you feel ready, I want you to show them to me."

"Okay."

"We're done here, aren't we?"

"Yes."

"About this job with Elizabeth…"

"I've promised her two weeks, Sam. And I'll be with her team more than with her. She'll be doing other things. What could happen in two weeks?"

He thought about the missions he'd endured in that length of time. "A lot can happen in two weeks, Moira. Two weeks can seem like an eternity."

He wove his way through the congested parking lot and turned the car toward his apartment.

He glanced at her to find her studying him, and to distract her said, "How about something to eat?"

"I'll be okay, Sam. If I feel the least bit uncomfortable, I'll tell her I can't work there and leave. I promise."

If he couldn't convince her not to work for Elizabeth, he could at least give her some instructions in how to watch her back.

At the apartment he lit the grill on his balcony while Moira made a salad.

"You hung the maps," she said when he came in.

"Yeah, it was a good idea. They suit me."

His phone rang and he slipped it free of his back pocket and glanced at the screen. "Hello."

"This is Detective Michael Hart of the San Diego PD. We'd like to talk to you about what happened on your boat. Would you be available in, say, an hour?"

"Yes." His glanced at Moira to find her watching him.

"We've been trying to contact Ms. McKee, but she hasn't answered her cell phone. Would you happen to know how we can contact her?"

"She's here with me."

"Great. We'd like to talk to her as well."

"She'll be here."

"We'll see you shortly."

Sam closed out the call. "That was Detective Hart. They'll be coming by soon. You may want to check your phone, because they've been trying to reach you."

DETECTIVE HART AND Buckler looked a little less careworn than they did the first time she met them. Hart's suit was freshly pressed, and Buckler was minus the dark stubble.

Buckler spoke first. "I'd like you to go back over what happened aboard your sailboat for me, Lieutenant Harding, while my partner talks to Ms. McKee."

"Can we step out onto the balcony to talk, Ms. McKee?" Detective Hart asked.

Sam's expression was neutral as she glanced his way. "Certainly." She led the way out on the small balcony taken up by Sam's grill and two chairs. The scent of grilled meat still lingered from the steaks he cooked earlier.

She waited for Detective Hart to speak. "The night of the charity dinner, what color was your dress, Ms. McKee?"

"It was cream-colored lace at the top and maroon satin for the skirt."

"Do you remember the color of Mrs. Clayborn's dress?"

"Yes. It was nearly the same as mine. Maybe just a half a shade darker. Though her dress was much more stylish than mine. We joked about it being a popular color."

"You said you saw a woman with Mark Travis outside late in the evening."

"Yes. At the corner of the building. He and the woman were in a passionate embrace."

"What color was her dress?"

"It was a little darker color than both mine and Mrs. Clayborn's, but in the same color family."

"Did you notice anyone else wearing a dress of that color?"

"There were a few others, but I didn't know any of them."

"Did you know Mark Travis?"

"No. Elizabeth introduced us that night." He didn't believe her.

"Would you be willing to sign off on allowing us to check the call history on your phone?"

"I don't have any problem with that."

He removed a paper from the folder he carried and extended paper and a pen. She signed it and returned both.

"I need to tell you there have been a few other incidents directed at those few other women who were wearing the same color you wore that night. There haven't been any more fatalities, but we believe the shooting on board the Gypsy is connected."

The man on the Jet Ski had been shooting at her. Her face and lips went numb.

Detective Buckler laid a hand on her arm. "You okay?"

She swallowed past the fear. "No, but I will be. Why is someone attacking women who wore maroon dresses to a charity dinner?"

"We haven't figured that out yet, but we're working on it."

"What about the woman Mark Travis was kissing that night?"

"We haven't been able to locate her yet. No one seems to know who she is."

"If I'd seen her face…I could have drawn her for you."

"I wish you had."

The conversation she and Sam shared played through her head. "I need to ask you something."

Hart's head shot up from his notes, and his expression sharpened with interest.

"Elizabeth Travis has asked me to do a painting for her and work with her team for a couple of weeks. Do you think I should back out of the arrangement until you've resolved this thing?"

He was silent a moment. "I think that might be a good idea, Ms. McKee."

"Okay. What can I do to protect myself?"

"I think this might be a good conversation for us to have with Lieutenant Harding and my partner."

She nodded. Sam would never say I told you so, but he would think it. He was used to living through dangerous situations, in dangerous places. He'd have some good ideas.

CHAPTER 16

M OIRA ADMIRED THE soring height of the ceiling that stretched
several floors. The modern chrome and glass railings of the
escalators and stairways gave an open, reflective feel to the space
and extended around the edge of a suspended second and third
floor.

"Up there is where I thought we'd hang the painting." Elizabeth pointed to the twelve-foot area beneath the posts and glass of
the railing. "It would place the painting front and center at the
entrance, where everyone walking in could view it."

"It would be perfect. And I've adjusted the design a little since
you saw it because I think it's important to include you in the
composition."

Moira fished around in her suitcase-size shoulder bag and
dragged out a sketchbook, flipping it open the reworked design,
and showed it to Elizabeth.

First came Elizabeth and Sarah together as she nursed her tiny
daughter, then Sarah at age eighteen months, then as an angel, as a
teenager, as a college graduate, as an adult, and with each transition she had grown and aged and looked as she would have if
she'd lived. As painful as it had to be for Elizabeth, Moira thought
it was beautiful.

Elizabeth remained silent for some time, then sighed. "It's
perfect. When can you start on it?"

"The canvas was delivered to my apartment two days ago, so I can start as soon as I get through with the meeting today. I wanted your approval with the design first."

"You have it." Elizabeth continued to study the drawing. "How did you know how to elongate her face and jaw as she aged?"

"I downloaded some software and age-progressed the picture you gave me, which made it very easy to draw her at different stages."

"It's amazing."

"I'm so glad you're pleased with it. I know the focus of the charity is on your daughter, but I wonder if you'd like to add your husband and son to the painting in any way?"

Elizabeth studied the drawing again. "No. It's always been about the lost potential of children, and though my husband's potential was cut short, it needs to focus on children. The design is perfect the way it is. It will be perfect for the space."

"Okay. I'll start the painting right away. I appreciate you allowing me to work from home instead of coming here."

"With technology we can hold conferences calls all over the world. Across town won't be a problem at all."

Sam stood by, his hands behind him in a sort of parade rest, his alert, eagle-eyed gaze scanning the lobby.

"My team is so eager to discuss projects with you, that I'd like to introduce you to them today. It's always easier to get a feel for someone face-to-face rather than over the phone, even with videoconferencing."

Elizabeth watched Sam's departure. "Sam has become a very attractive man. He was handsome as a boy as well, but there's something very virile about him now, and very intense. I noticed it at the dinner that night. It makes for a very complicated man, doesn't it?"

Moira didn't know how to reply. She'd never been one to share her feelings with anyone, let alone a stranger. She settled for speaking in the abstract. "I think complicated can be a challenge, attractive and very interesting, don't you?"

Elizabeth's smile was wistful. "And never boring. Because they have so many sides to their personality."

Was she speaking from experience? Had her husband been like Sam? Intense, controlled, passionate, tender, caring, protective, the list went on and on. But she didn't believe Sam would ever be unfaithful. His experience as a boy had been too painful. If he ever wanted to be with someone else, he'd come to her and tell her.

Elizabeth broke into her thoughts. "You're very lucky to have found him."

"Yes, I am. You're partly responsible for our being together. If I hadn't come to the dinner that night, we might never have met."

Elizabeth smiled. "You're welcome."

Moira chuckled.

"Ready to meet the team?"

"Yes."

"Is Sam going to hang out until after the meeting?"

"No. He's going to come back and pick me up. I'll go tell him we're going up to start."

Moira crossed the lobby, and his gaze homed in on her in a way that made her heart tumble. Elizabeth was right, she was very lucky. "I'm not sure how long we'll be."

"Just call when you want to be picked up."

"I will."

"Remember the plan. You don't go anywhere in the building by yourself."

"I won't. I'll be in the room with Elizabeth's team most of the time."

"Stay aware of your surroundings and where everyone is. I've spoken to security about what happened at the boat, so they'll be keeping an eye on you."

"I'm not sure I want to say thanks to that. It seems a bit creepy to have someone watching all the time."

"Better safe than sorry." He brushed her cheek with a kiss. "Call when you want to be picked up. And wait for me inside the building."

He'd gone over and over those things. "I will."

As they got in the elevator Elizabeth asked, "How long can Sam play bodyguard?"

"Not long." Just these two days. "He has too many other responsibilities. But now school's out, I'll be staying home painting, so I'll be fine."

"How long will the painting take?"

"Possibly a week, ten days at the most. The canvas is large, and keeping the color and details true is the important thing. I'm going to maintain that wispy, impressionistic look I showed you in the pastel drawing throughout."

"It's going to be beautiful."

They reached the third floor and the elevator door opened. Until that moment Moira had been distracted, but now nerves made her stomach jitter and she was having trouble taking in a complete breath.

They walked down a long hall to an office with glass walls, like a large aquarium, where ten people sat in the clustered easy chairs, tablets at the ready.

Since planning the entire fundraising processes had come a little at a time, talking about everything she and the teachers did as a whole was complex. She made notes to help her break each thing down and include the processes they'd used to do it. It had taken numerous committees and an army of students.

Work the problem was Sam's mantra. She'd dealt with worse things, using the same idea: one element at a time.

As she entered the room, Elizabeth said, "Good morning, everyone."

Conversations ended and they turned their attention to Elizabeth at once.

She waited until she and Moira reached the front of the room before saying, "This is Moira McKee. She's a local artist and teacher, but she's also a brilliant planner. I've already told you how much money she and her school raised for Sarah's Dreams. She's going to explain how they did it. My idea is to create a fundraising packet to encourage other schools to do the same, not only for Sarah's Dreams, but for their school's needs as well. What Moira did was a school-wide project that included every department and opened the entire school population to an economic and creative learning process that benefited them educationally and benefited our charity economically. Please welcome her."

Every eye in the room turned on her, and Moira felt the pressure of their attention. She remembered that first day at school when she was first hired, when Mr. Jacobs introduced her to the student body. Her hundred-and-seventy-pound body had felt heavy as lead as she walked across the stage to the podium and said hello. It had taken every ounce of courage to say just a few words. She'd carried a weight of shame about how she looked then that was just as heavy as the physical pounds. She'd allowed the many slights and cuts to diminish her in ways she still had to work hard to overcome.

It seemed surreal that people were looking to her for something other than a painting or an art history lesson.

Her body was considerably lighter now as she walked to the table and withdrew her notes and the packets she'd created for Elizabeth's team. She smiled, and felt the release of nerves when everyone smiled back.

"I've tried to consolidate what we did to make it easier for everyone." She walked among them, handing out the booklets. "If you'll open them, we'll take it step-by-step, and you can ask me questions as we go."

SAM WOKE TO the distant sound of a police siren. He glanced toward the alarm clock. Four-thirty came earlier and earlier it seemed. He wanted to snuggle up to Moira and go back to sleep, but things were winding back up for the SEAL trainees.

For those who had survived Hell Week they'd been doing bobbing, drown-proofing, more PT, and Red Cross lifesaving instruction. And at least there were only thirty-three candidates left, so it would be easier to keep track of them.

Moira turned on her side toward him, her hand resting palm up between them. Her pale features, relaxed in sleep, appeared young and vulnerable and so beautiful.

She'd been painting when he went to bed, but he woke up when she climbed into bed beside him about two. She was as driven as he was, and her talent was amazing. He'd been impressed by the other drawings and paintings, but what she was doing on the huge canvas in her living room had reached a whole other level.

In order not to wake her, he eased out of bed and gathered his clothes, and used the small bathroom off the living room to shave and dress, then fixed some coffee.

In the middle of writing himself a note to pick up more coffee on the way home, it hit him.

He was hooked.

His first thought in the mornings was of her, his last thought at night was the same. He wanted her every time he laid hands on her. Hell, he wanted her every time she looked at him. She was giving and passionate and caring. She had opened his world to things besides work and his team. She'd embraced his team like they were family. And she made him happy.

He was hooked. And it felt right.

He wanted to take his clothes off, climb back in bed, and make love to her right now, but she'd only been asleep two hours and needed to rest. But he couldn't resist going back to the bedroom. He stood at the door and studied every angle of her face. Her eyelids had a bluish tint, while the red of her lashes fanned against her pale skin. Everything about her was vibrant and unusual. He eased into the room, knelt by the bed, and brushed a kiss against her forehead.

He wanted to wake her and tell her to be extra careful. She was staying home, trusting him to do the shopping, but she couldn't hide out in the apartment twenty-four seven. She had her school in-services coming up, an eye exam appointment, numerous small things she'd want to take care of herself.

The cops needed to get with the program and figure out who was responsible for Mark Travis and Denise Clayborn's deaths and the attacks on Moira and the other women. A phone call to Detective Buckler and Hart was in their immediate future.

He glanced at his watch. Duty called, and he had never felt less like answering.

Moira padded into the kitchen, her eyes heavy. Her hair stood up in all directions, and the wild, burnished curls looked sexy as hell.

"I didn't wake you, did I?" he asked.

"No." She took the cup of coffee from his hand and took a sip. "Whoa. That could stand without the cup." She handed it back to him.

Sam chuckled. "It's not coffee, it's starter fluid." He pulled her close. "I have to go. You need to go back to bed."

"I will." She laid her head against his chest.

Sam smoothed her wild curls, releasing the scent of her vanilla shampoo. He breathed it in. "Is the painting done?"

"Yes. I thought I'd call Elizabeth and tell her it can be picked up this morning."

"That's great! You're very fast."

"I wanted to get it done so I can move on to other things. I have one more meeting at her office complex with the team, then my break is my own."

"Good. When's the meeting?"

"Friday of next week."

"I'll see if I can get off to go with you, Moira."

"I'll be fine. I'll be with the team the whole time, and I'll have security walk me to my car when I get ready to leave for home."

He still didn't like the idea. "I have a meeting after we release the candidates for the weekend, so I might be an hour late. We'll do something tonight to celebrate the completion of the painting."

"I'd like that."

"Leave it to me." He brushed her lips with a kiss. "I'll see you later."

"Okay."

On the way out he paused in front of the painting that stretched against one wall of the living room. The painting of Elizabeth Travis and her infant daughter was so lifelike it looked like a photograph. The other images of Sarah grew fainter and fainter as she aged and moved through the life she'd missed. The painting was about lost dreams, and it represented them very well.

He'd be glad when it was delivered to Elizabeth Travis and Moira's connection to the woman was over. He wanted her to paint something that inspired her, something that reflected her positive attitude and her humor.

He tore off a scrap of paper from a drawing pad, wrote a short note, propped it against the clay bowl on her coffee table, and locked the door behind him.

THE WATER FELT wonderful and Moira started out at a crawl as she swam the length of the pool and back. Her muscles warmed, a surge of endorphins hit her system, and she dug deeper but kept that same slow, easy pace. She rolled her head to the right, took a breath, and kept going. By the fifteenth lap she felt the burn and continued for five more laps, then rolled onto her back to backstroke to the stairs.

She just put her key in to unlock her apartment door when her cell phone rang.

As soon as she put the phone to her ear, Elizabeth Travis said, "The painting is fabulous. Truly remarkable."

It was always so difficult for her to deal with the praise people gave her for her work. "I'm so glad you're pleased with it."

"Building maintenance has already hung it, and I'd love for you to come see it. I thought we'd do an unveiling later in the week and have the press here. Would you be up for that?"

"I'd love to be at the unveiling and see how everyone reacts."

"Good. I can't tell you how pleased I am. It's a powerful piece, and will represent the charity beautifully. The emotions you captured are amazing."

"I only painted what I saw. The picture you gave me of you and Sarah was the inspiration."

"Thank you."

The quiver in Elizabeth's voice had her own eyes pricking with tears.

"I know it's late, but I'd like you to come and see how the crew has hung it and let me thank you face-to-face while I cut you a check for your work. You more than earned your commission. It will only take a few minutes."

Moira hesitated. Sam was due home in a couple of hours, and she wanted to shower and dress. "I just got out of the pool. I can be there in half an hour."

"Good. I'll be in my office on the second floor. The staff are almost all gone, but I'll leave the door downstairs unlocked. Just come on up when you get here."

She'd done the right thing in turning Elizabeth down for the job. As nice as Elizabeth was, and as much as she admired her, there was a pushiness in the way she dealt with things. If Moira had worked with her, they'd have clashed and she'd have had to quit. It was a relief to have the commission finished so she could move on.

Twenty minutes later, after a quick shower and a change of clothes, she grabbed her keys and shut the door behind her. She was in the car when she thought about Sam. If he got home earlier than expected, he'd wonder where she was.

She paused before starting the car and texted him. He'd probably be with either the BUD/S guys or his commanding officer for the meeting he mentioned. He wouldn't answer his texts until he was finished. She'd probably be back by the time he got home.

Home. He'd been staying with her for ten days, and seemed to have settled in. Did he realize how much she loved having him there, sharing her bed and her life?

He made everything seem so casual. But it wasn't casual for her. It had never been casual for her. If she told him how she felt, would he pull away?

She gnawed on the problem all the way to the Sarah's Dreams

headquarters. When she pushed the door open, the lobby was empty, the hustle and bustle of the building during work hours missing.

What dominated the space was the large canvas hung from the second story railing and covered by a tarp.

The faint sound of some kind of machine running down one of the halls reached her. As she crossed the lobby to the stairs, the rubber soles of her shoes squeaked on the highly polished tile.

The second floor held numerous offices, and she passed several that had the lights off, the doors shut. At the end of the wide hallway were the double doors of Elizabeth's office. She knocked at the panel and waited for permission to enter.

Elizabeth opened the door and smiled. "I'm so glad you could meet with me. Come in."

SAM GLANCED AT his watch as Lt. Commander Hawk Yazzie finally called the meeting to order. "I just want to go over some base violations I've been made aware of recently. Just when you think you have protocols in place for every instance, some frogman gets creative and screws everything up.

"I did a quick inspection of some of the base equipment cages and realized there were some additions to those facilities that go beyond the scope of requisitioned military equipment, and I'm not talking about beer."

That got a chuckle from most of the guys.

"I realize we all spend more time here at our home away from home than we do our real ones, but we can't really decide to decorate the place like a bachelor's pad either."

Sam looked up. Shit! He'd inspected their cages and found Sheila, the name all the guys had voted on for the red headed bombshell in the painting.

"Personal pictures are to be secured in lockers, out of sight."

They'd hung Sheila inside one of the cages, hidden beneath a couple of flak jackets. Obviously they hadn't covered her well enough. Word of the painting had traveled fast, and some of the other teams had shown up to get a look at her as well as the team drawing.

"That being said, team morale means everything, and what works for one team, may work for them all. Then it becomes a tradition."

Moira had done the painting for his eight-man team. There were six platoons of two teams. That would mean she'd have to do eleven more paintings. Shit!

"There would have to be a financial investment to make that happen." Hawk said. "That would be up to the individual teams."

He was throwing Moira a bone, so they weren't getting a slap on the wrists for bending a regulation. But they'd have to secure the Sheila painting more carefully in the future. In fact, he'd buy a cabinet to go in one of the cages to house it.

The men shifted into serious mode as Hawk moved on to something more important.

When the meeting broke up, Sam switched on his phone to find several new texts. One from Tim, one from Alisha, two from his mother, and one from Moira. He scanned through them quickly. Finding Moira had gone to the charity headquarters alone kicked in that niggling concern of his.

Hawk flagged him down on his way out. "Please tell Moira that Zoe is so crazy about the painting we've hung it in the bedroom. Now she wants one done of me. I'll be getting back to Moira about that."

Sam nodded. "I'll pass that on. She'll be thrilled Zoe liked it. She's just finished a huge canvas for Sarah's Dreams headquarters. It was hung today."

"Congratulate her on that as well."

"Roger that, sir."

"About the other painting."

"I'll secure it, sir."

"Good."

"As for the pencil drawing of your team, I believe that would be acceptable to leave in in full view, Sam."

He was relieved to hear that. "Thank you, sir."

"How's Book?"

Anxious to call Moira, and the itchy, hyper-aware feeling he got during tense situations worked its way over the back of his neck. If he could hear her voice and know she was being careful, it would relieve it.

But Sam resigned himself to staying a few more minutes to fill his commanding officer in on Book's progress.

"I THOUGHT WE could lift the tarp the maintenance crew laid over the painting so you can see how they've mounted it." Elizabeth led the way down the hall. The white, calf-length, summer skirt she wore flowed around her legs, feminine and lovely. Moira felt like an underdressed slob in her lightweight slacks and cotton blouse.

In the commons area on the second-floor landing, two large, pale green sofas faced one another with a big acrylic coffee table between them. They passed the arrangement and went to the railing.

"I can get a good enough idea of placement without raising the tarp, Elizabeth. It looks as though your maintenance crew has done an excellent job securing it, otherwise the weight of the tarp would be causing a problem."

"But I want you to see it revealed from the floor below. It's very striking. If you can help me lift the tarp, even at one end, you'll get the effect."

With a six-thousand-dollar check tucked securely in her purse, she could afford to do what the client wanted.

"If you'll get that end," Elizabeth said pointing toward the left.

Moira dropped her purse at her feet, leaned over the railing, and started gathering the tarp. The railing tilted forward and she grabbed the support.

She heard a cry behind her and was suddenly shoved hard against the railing. She grabbed at the metal post but only got a handful of tarp that slid with her. The banister shook, and one side broke loose.

Moira screamed and caught the frame of the canvas just in time to keep from tumbling over the edge. The heavy tempered glass fell, hit the floor, and shattered, the sound explosive. The open space twenty feet below yawned before her.

She clung to the canvas and dropped to one knee as a wave of vertigo hit her.

"Why did you kill my husband?"

Moira dragged her attention away from the drop and turned to look directly into the barrel of the black pistol Elizabeth pointed at her.

Moira's stomach plummeted and she fought back a wave of nausea.

Elizabeth stepped closer. "Why?"

SAM SLID BEHIND the wheel of his SUV and reached for his phone, hitting Moira's number and waiting for her to pick up. The phone rang several times, then went to voice mail. If she was home she'd have answered. If she was still talking to Elizabeth, she might have turned her phone off.

He glanced at his watch again. It was nearly seven. She should have made it home by now. Ever since she was nearly shot on the boat, he'd been unable to shake off this hyper feeling of concern. There was someone out there who meant to harm her.

They had both assumed it was a man. Because of the black wet suit, the gun, he had also assumed it was a man. Plus he was more used to being shot at by men.

But it could have been a woman. It could have been Elizabeth Travis. What if she was out to kill every woman who'd slept with her husband? What if she assumed Moira was one of them?

Those thoughts had gone through his mind more than once. Dammit.

He decided to swing by the charity's headquarters since it was on the way to her apartment and see if Moira's car was still in the parking lot. If she was still there, he'd go in and find her.

HOW COULD ELIZABETH believe she killed him? She hadn't even known Mark Travis. "I didn't kill him, Elizabeth. He was dead when I found him."

"He was below your room. He had to fall from your balcony."

"I don't know where he fell from, but it wasn't from my balcony. Sam was with me all night. The last time we saw him was outside the hotel on the sidewalk that leads down to the beach."

Elizabeth shoved the pistol barrel at her for emphasis. "You're lying."

"You introduced us, Elizabeth. I never spoke to him again. After meeting Sam that night, no one else could measure up to him. Not for me. We haven't been apart longer than a day since we met."

She saw the uncertainly in the woman's gaze, then suddenly the expression shifted into something harder. "It had to be you. You're the only one it could be. He was with a woman in a maroon dress."

"The other woman's dress wasn't maroon. It was wine—deeper, darker. The material had a shimmer to it where it seemed to shift shades. And she was young, very slender."

Elizabeth's eyes widened. "How do you know that?"

"Sam and I saw him with her as we walked down to the beach."

The door opened below, but Moira didn't dare take her eyes off the pistol. "It wasn't me, Elizabeth."

Moira caught movement from the stairs out of the corner of her eye.

"Mom?" Michael Travis's voice was strained with uncertainty.

"Stay away, Michael."

"Mom…what are you doing?"

"She killed your father, Michael. She slept with him."

"No, Mom." He approached Elizabeth like he was walking on eggshells. "She was with that Sam dude."

"How do you know that?"

"Because I saw them walking down to the beach together from our room."

"You were at your prom. You couldn't have seen them."

"I went back to the hotel early."

Tears streamed down his face. "Mom… He was screwing my girlfriend. My *sixteen-year-old* girlfriend. I told him to stay away from her, for once in his life to do the right thing, but he wouldn't listen.

"Nina and I had a fight about it. It was Nina he was with that night. She left and must have called him to pick her up. When I got back to the Del, she was with him. I walked in on them. Dad told her to get dressed and he called her a cab to take her home. It was like nothing had happened.

After she left I told him I was going to call the police. He'd be charged with statutory rape. He'd go to jail. And I'd be glad. I was so sick of him sleeping around and rubbing it in your face. Rubbing it in *my* face."

He wiped his shirtsleeve across his wet face. "Instead of the police, I dialed Nina's number and threatened to tell her parents. He slapped me, and I just went crazy. I hit him, and he staggered back and hit his head on one of the posts that held the roof. He struggled with me, trying to take the phone away from me. We fell against the railing and then he just went over. He was there one second and just gone the next. I climbed down over the balcony and dropped to the ground below to help, but he was…his neck…"

His face paled and a fine mist of sweat shown on his forehead. "He was already dead and I think I went a little crazy. I just ran to my car and drove away. I went home and got drunk but I knew I had to be back at the hotel before morning. I don't know how I made it back to the Del without wrecking the car. I slept for a while in the parking lot, when I woke up, it was still dark, so I staggered in and went to my room. When the police came and woke you up to tell you he was dead, I was puking my guts up."

Michael turned toward Moira. "I'm sorry you had to find him like that. I'm sorry my mom threatened you."

Elizabeth had done more than that. The broken railing had been tampered with. Elizabeth had obviously loosened the bolts that held it in place. And she had shoved Moira against it from behind, intending to kill her. If she'd fallen she'd have been killed or severely injured.

Elizabeth turned to face Moira, her face slack with shock and grief. Moira eased to her feet and reached for her purse.

"You can't leave." Elizabeth raised the gun again.

The doors below opened again. Elizabeth shifted the gun away from Moira to the person who walked in, and Moira knew without looking that it was Sam.

Elizabeth would shoot him. He was more of a threat than she was.

Moira lunged at Elizabeth, tackling the woman. The gun went off. One of the glass panels shattered. Moira clawed at Elizabeth's wrist as the gun swung wildly toward the stairs as Sam bound up them.

Michael was suddenly there helping her hold down his mother. "Mom don't do this. It's over. You have to let it be over. Please."

Sam wrenched the gun out of Elizabeth's grasp, and the woman let out a frustrated shriek.

Moira staggered to her feet, and Sam caught her around the waist to steady her.

Elizabeth curled into a ball and covered her face with her hands. "What will we do?" Sobs shook her shoulders. "What will we do?"

Tears ran down Michael's face again. "Whatever comes next, Mom." The pain in his face aged him.

He no longer looked like a boy when he took his mother into his arms and rocked her.

CHAPTER 17

INSIDE THE BACK seat of the detectives' car, Sam kept an arm around Moira. She'd been white and shaky when he hustled out of the building, and she'd calmed somewhat, but the trauma still lingered.

"Elizabeth was always so polite and cordial, but there was an edge to it. And she was a little pushy. I was glad I'd turned down the job she offered me, but the commission for the painting was too much to pass up." Moira's words sounded a little slurred, and she looked a bit shocky. He tightened his arm around her to share his body heat.

Detectives Buckler and Hart came out of the headquarters building with both Elizabeth and Michael in handcuffs and put them in separate police cars for transport.

"I spent all that time and thought working on that painting, and she probably hired me to do it just to create the opportunity to…" Her voice dwindled away.

"I think she probably hired you originally for all the right reasons, Moira. Your talent is tremendous. Anyone who sees your work would have to be blind not to recognize that."

She stilled and rested her head against his shoulder. "Why did you decide to stop by here?"

"I've been pushing around the idea that the person on the Jet Ski who shot at you could possibly have been a woman instead of a man. We both saw a black wet suit and a black gun. And I guess the black seemed more masculine than feminine. But Elizabeth had a better motive to kill Mark than anyone else involved with him, and she had a better motive to kill the women he may have slept with. Also, she was trying too hard to get close to you with the concert, and then the offer of the job and the painting commission. I just didn't trust her."

"But she wasn't the one who killed Mark. It was Michael."

Sam's jaw tightened. "I understand the rage he felt at the way Mark was behaving. I've felt it myself toward my own father."

"And he was more than provoked. His father struck him first. But his fall was an accident."

"And he'd just caught him groping his sixteen-year-old girl-friend." And jealousy could have played a part in their fight.

"His father was a sexual predator, or maybe a sex addict. And you were right, Michael and Elizabeth knew about all the women. He flaunted his behavior in front them both, and going after Michael's girlfriend smacks of deliberate provocation. It would have been better if Elizabeth had divorced her husband rather than force Michael to live with his father's depravities. Your mother was wise to have separated you from your father."

"I'll tell her you said that."

She curled against him and gave another shudder. "I want to go home, Sam."

His arm tightened around her. He wanted to take her there. She had come close to dying twice today. First from the fall Elizabeth had planned for her, and again when the woman pointed a loaded gun at her.

He owed Michael a debt for talking his mother down. He could have lost Moira before he had a chance to tell her what she meant to him.

He was the one who ran toward danger. Moira wasn't sup-posed to be the one in the line of fire. Frustration and relief tumbled together inside him.

Buckler sauntered toward the car, rested an arm on the open car door, and leaned down to look into the vehicle. "I know you've been through a trauma, but we'd appreciate it if you could come down to the station and give us a formal statement, Ms. McKee. The more information we have about what went on here today, the more thorough our questioning will be of Mrs. Travis and her son."

"Okay."

"You two can ride with me, and I'll arrange for a car to drop you back here to pick up your vehicles if you like."

"They're denying everything, aren't they?" she asked.

"Michael is being cooperative about his father's death. Mrs. Travis is being less than forthcoming. But we have the gun, and it may be the key to getting her to talk."

The gun would likely tie Elizabeth to the shooting on the boat, and possibly Denise Clayborn's death. Had Denise slept with Mark Travis? Sam couldn't imagine her doing something like that.

Had Elizabeth really hunted down the other women at the dinner who'd worn maroon dresses because she thought one of them was responsible for Mark's death? She must have, because she'd accused Moira of having slept with him and of killing him.

The whole thing was fucked up.

MOIRA TOSSED HER purse and keys on the table by the door and collapsed on the couch. Sam was close behind her. "Two hours to give a statement was ridiculous," she complained.

"Yeah, it was. How about I fix us both a deep glass of wine and we can get drunk together?" he asked.

"Don't tempt me. I'll just wake up in the morning with a headache. Let's order something to eat and have it delivered."

Her cell phone rang, and she groaned as she dragged herself to her feet and retrieved it from her purse. It was an SDPD number. She answered it.

"Moira." Detective Buckler's voice sounded as tired as she felt. "From the evidence our team has been able to collect, it all backs up your statement. Elizabeth Travis is going to be charged with attempted murder. When ballistics comes back, I have an idea she'll be facing murder charges."

"Denise Clayborn?"

"I'm not at liberty to discuss an ongoing investigation, but I wish we could have warned her."

"It didn't do any good to warn me. I never had a clue Elizabeth was so unbalanced.

"What will happen to Michael?" She had such sympathy for the young man, and everything he'd been through with both parents. And besides, Michael's actions had saved her life. She already made sure to put that in her statement, hoping it would help him in some way.

"It will be up to the DA what charges he will face. Manslaughter, or it may be ruled an accident."

"Please tell him how Michael helped me."

"I'll include it in my notes."

Relief had her drawing a deep breath. "Thank you for updating me."

"You're welcome. Try and have a good evening."

"We will." She collapsed onto the couch a second time.

Sam was silent for a moment. "When we first met, I never would have guessed what a strong woman you are, Moira."

She'd never considered herself strong. "You probably thought I was a pushover." She had jumped into bed with him so quickly.

"But you dealt with finding a dead body. And all the responsibility your principal piled on you, all the work you've done with Book, and…" He paused his expression blank with some powerful emotion." Being shot at on the boat and today the way you dealt with Elizabeth Travis and the police afterward. You're a strong lady."

There was a note of something in his voice she couldn't quite decipher. She studied his face, trying to read what he was getting at.

His tawny gaze looked deep into hers, the gold surrounding his irises expanding. "You know the wives of SEALs have to be strong ladies. They have to take charge of everything while we're deployed."

He said wives, not girlfriends. Her heart began to pound in her throat and wrists. "I'm sure they do."

"I left you a note this morning before I left. You didn't find, it did you?"

His sudden change of subject gave her emotional whiplash. "No, where is it?"

"Sitting right in front of you on the coffee table."

The scrap of paper was propped up against the clay bowl she kept there. She laughed and reached for it. It had her name written across it in bold, manly handwriting.

That was Sam. Bold and manly, hard-ass Harding with everyone—except her and his mother, of course.

She unfolded the note and read, *You know how hard it is for me to say the words. I thought writing them would be easier, and then you'd have it in black and white, tangible proof.*

In bigger letters he'd written. *I love you. Sam.*

Tears blurred her vision. She held the paper close against her and let the tears fall. "I love you, too. I have since you punched your brother for insulting me. I don't think I ever felt I'd be worthy of love unless I changed myself, my life." She turned to straddle his lap after carefully setting the note on the end table. She cupped Sam's face in her hands and kissed him softly, tenderly, showing him how much she loved him. His hands gripped her hips and she broke the kiss. "On the boat, when you helped me dress after we made love, I felt loved, and I hoped…"

"If something had happened to you…I would have always regretted not telling you how I felt." His eyes darkened with emotion. "You've changed my life, Moira. I was closed off from people. You've helped me learn to be more open with you, my men, my family. My life is richer for having you in it. I love you. I want you with me as much as possible, so when we're apart, when I have to deploy, we'll have moments like this to hold on to and keep what we feel for each other strong."

Moira felt lighter than she had in hours. She didn't have to hear him say the words when the evidence of how he felt about her was right there in the way he held her. In the way his hands caressed her back. In the way he looked at her when they made love. In the way he was looking at her right now.

He'd been telling her how he felt all along. Actions said more than words. But hearing the words sure felt good. Her heart seemed to swell every time he said it. "Just say it one more time."

Sam skimmed his hand around the back of her neck and drew her lips to his. "I love you," he said against them. And when he proceeded to show her, she was more than happy to do the same.

THE END

FOR MORE INFORMATION ABOUT TERESA REASOR

Website: www.teresareasor.com

MILITARY ROMANTIC SUSPENSE
BREAKING FREE (Book 1 of the SEAL Team Heartbreakers)
BREAKING THROUGH (Book 2 of the SEAL Team Heartbreakers)
BREAKING AWAY (Book 3 of the SEAL Team Heartbreakers)
BREAKING TIES (A SEAL Team Heartbreakers Novella)
BUILDING TIES (Book 4 of the SEAL Team Heartbreakers)
BREAKING BOUNDARIES (Book 5 of the SEAL Team
Heartbreakers)
BREAKING OUT (BOOK 6 of the SEAL Team Heartbreakers)
BREAKING POINT (A SEAL Team Heartbreakers Novella)
BREAKING HEARTS (Book 7 of the SEAL Team Heartbreakers)
BREAKING CHAINS (Book 8 of the SEAL Team Heartbreakers)
BUILDING STRENGTH (Book 9 of the SEAL Team Heartbreakers)

SEALS IN PARADISE SERIES
HOT SEAL, RUSTY NAIL
HOT SEAL, ROMAN NIGHTS
HOT SEAL, TAKING THE PLUNGE (Coming September 1, 2020)

PARANORMAL ROMANCE
TIMELESS
DEEP WITHIN THE SHADOWS (Book 1 of the Superstition Series)
DEEP WITHIN THE STONE (Book 2 of the Superstition Series)
DEEP WITHIN THE MIND (Book 3 of the Superstition Series)
WHISPER IN MY EAR
HAVE WAND, WILL TRAVEL (Book 1 Have Wand, Will Travel)
ONCE BITTEN, TWICE SHY (Book 2 Have Wand, Will Travel)
ADVENTURES OF A WITCHY WALLFLOWER (Book 3 Have
Wand, Will Travel)

HISTORICAL ROMANCE
CAPTIVE HEARTS
HIGHLAND MOONLIGHT
TO CAPTURE A HIGHLANDER'S HEART: THE TRILOGY

The Highland Moonlight Spinoff Trilogy in parts
TO CAPTURE A HIGHLANDER'S HEART: THE BEGINNING
TO CAPTURE A HIGHLANDER'S HEART: THE COURTSHIP
TO CAPTURE A HIGHLANDER'S HEART: THE WEDDING NIGHT

SHORT STORIES
AN AUTOMATED DEATH: A STEAMPUNK SHORT STORY
CAUGHT IN THE ACT: A HUMOROUS SHORT STORY

CHILDREN'S BOOK
WILLY C. SPARKS, THE DRAGON WHO LOST HIS FIRE

www.ingramcontent.com/pod-product-compliance
Lightning Source LLC
Chambersburg PA
CBHW022102170626
46808CB00002B/560